The Hermit

Eugène Ionesco

The Hermit

TRANSLATED FROM THE FRENCH
BY RICHARD SEAVER

A RICHARD SEAVER BOOK
THE VIKING PRESS : NEW YORK

Kramerbooks

The Hermit

At thirty-five, it's high time to quit the rat race. Assuming there is a rat race. I was sick and tired of my job. It was already late: I was fast approaching forty. If I hadn't come into that unexpected inheritance I would have died of depression and boredom. They are admittedly few and far between, but a handful of American uncles still do exist. Unless mine was the last. In any case, none of my colleagues in the little office where I worked had an American father, cousin, or uncle. They did a poor job of concealing their jealousy: imagine, not having to work any longer! My good-byes were quickly done. I offered to buy a round of farewell drinks at the corner café, Beaujolais was the drink I offered. I hadn't even invited Juliette. She was always upset or annoyed about one thing or another. After having abandoned ourselves to each other's charms, we had finally simply abandoned each other. The boss was even more annoyed than my girl friend. Ex-girl friend. He had been expecting something like this, he said to me. Strange, for I hadn't been expecting it myself. I should have given three months' notice, he said. Those were the rules, he assured me. "I'm going to have a great deal of trouble finding somebody like you." I thought of all the times when he had berated me about my work, periodically threatening to fire me, each time making me tremble in my boots, for where would I ever have found the same job as the one to which, however poorly, I had grown accustomed? Each time that he threatened to fire me, fear inspired me to a burst of activity that lasted for two or three days. And then the fire died down. About two weeks later, new threats. So it was that I worked hard roughly six or seven days every month. It was exhausting. I wasn't going to give my boss one day more, that was my revenge. I gladly would have paid him my month's penalty. In the long run, he refused to accept it, to show what a nice fellow he was. I'm not mean. I allowed him that one satisfaction.

I nonetheless went to see Jeanine, the cashier: "So you're leaving us . . . now that you're wealthy. . . . You really don't want to live in this part of town any more? . . . Where are you going to set up housekeeping? . . . I don't see how you can do it by yourself, you're all thumbs, poor man. . . . Oh, of course, now you can afford a maid." She had tears in her eyes. For a brief interlude, she had taken Juliette's place in my affections. But that was already a long time ago. Grown used to sitting for hours on end at the cash register, she could no longer move. She was growing fat. She knew that I was not like everyone else, that I was an ungrateful wretch. And yet I am like everyone else, like all the others, skeptical, disillusioned, both wearying and weary, living a life without purpose, working as little as possible—because there was no choice—an epicurean in my own way: good food and drink, to help me from time to time to leave behind the universal bitterness and lassitude.

To my surprise, the boss did come to the café for the farewell drink. Lucienne came too. She was the third-ranking employee in the office, a person of some importance: "management." She came with Pierre Ramboule. Lucienne had been my third and final love affair. Because of our office hours, and the fact that most of the employees lived in the suburbs, we didn't have too much time to play Don Juan, so we settled for what was available on the premises. We took what came our way. She—I'm referring to Lucienne—was the one whom I had loved the most, if I may use the term, no other strikes me at the moment. She had thrown me over for this Pierre Ramboule, at the time a recent arrival among us, who had youth going for him. Lucienne was the youngest of the three, and the only one with a nice body. She had been seduced by Pierre, a young man full of vinegar and great ambitions: he planned to work in our office for only a short period of time, he explained, for the experience. He was expecting important sums of money, and when they arrived he would go into business on his own, big business. He had led Lucienne to believe that she was part of his future plans, both private and professional. It was now exactly five years and one month since the boss had hired Pierre Ramboule, and exactly five years since Lucienne had thrown me over for him. Both of them were still there. "You can make this a double celebration," I said to Lucienne as she came into the café. "You can also celebrate your fifth anniversary."

Lucienne blushed; she was always embarrassed to see me, and since she saw me every day I saw her blush daily. She had slight pangs of conscience at having thrown me over, and she was sorry she had so misjudged Pierre, who had turned out to be no better than I. To tell the truth, I'm not the ugliest fellow who ever lived; it's simply that my face has that washed-out, faded look, having lost its freshness at birth. And then there are my washed-out blue eyes.

The dirty trick that Lucienne had played on me had hurt me deeply. I'll never find anyone else as pretty, anyone with such nice legs and beautiful posture, anyone with a smile so winning. I had done a lot of soul-searching when she left me, I didn't know where to turn. I had come to realize that Lucienne had occupied a place in my life which I had been unaware of as long as she had been there. I had even gone into a depression and taken a month's sick leave, which I had spent in parts of town far away from where I worked. Actually, it had only been a question of double solitude. I saw that now. But at the time of my despair, I felt that I had lost paradise. Ahead of me I saw nothing but torpor and confusion, and told myself so. Was she any better off with him now?

On one hand, Pierre no longer spoke of future projects he planned to take on; on the other hand, he had taken on a paunch. He too seemed embarrassed whenever he met me; oh, not all that much . . . after five years, how much can remain of a drama that was ordinary and ridiculous to begin with? Perhaps neither of them felt embarrassed upon seeing me. Perhaps it was all in my mind. The fact remains that for five years I hadn't been with a woman. I had grown used to living alone. Too untrusting to try to live my own life, as the saying goes, or to build, or rebuild, my life. Had I in fact ever had a life? With Lucienne, a vague beginning of something . . . with Juliette too, perhaps: a spot of blue sky among the clouds.

We drank a first glass of Beaujolais, a second glass of Beaujolais, a third glass of Beaujolais. Before I ordered a fourth round, the boss left. He wished me good luck, but not before he had gone to great lengths to tell me about his plans to enlarge the business, and said that he had some very interesting ideas up his sleeve, that the number of his customers was growing by leaps and bounds, that he didn't know how to cope with the influx of orders, and that he was going to have to take on additional employees. It made me tremble to think of all the work I would have had to do if I had stayed on . . . but thanks to my uncle in America. . . The boss wanted to triple, quadruple his volume of business. That meant I would have had to work three or four times harder. Then when I gave it some thought I didn't really believe him; business was doubtless going to go on much as before, that is, not too badly but not too well either. I carefully avoided another potential danger: he didn't offer to let me invest in his business. I realized that he didn't want me to. His business was meant to remain small. He was afraid to take risks. He was obviously right; why knock yourself out? In his place I wouldn't have acted any differently. Pierre and Lucienne left with the others, after the fifth round. Everybody was slightly tipsy. Needless to say, I promised to come back and see them from time to time because, after all, fifteen years working in one place wasn't exactly to be sneezed at. I had seen most of the employees in the company arrive, and more than a few depart. I had known the boss's father, from whom the son had taken over just when I had started to work there. As she left, Lucienne gave me a smile, tinged with regret it seemed to me, perhaps even remorse. Goodness, she had a white hair; she also had a wrinkle or two. Amazing; I had never thought she could be anything but young forever. Did she have a tear in the corner of her eye as she blew me a kiss with her warm lips? We had no reason to be angry with each other. She was naïve enough to think perhaps that with me love might not have ended on the rocks. Perhaps she was telling herself it still wasn't too late; if I was willing, maybe we could start all over again. Or she might think it was the lack of money, the dull, anonymous work routine that had nipped our life in the bud; but love can move mountains, love can burst all bonds, even steel; nothing can stand in its way, as we all know. It's our own mediocrity that makes us let go of love, makes us renounce it. True Love doesn't know the meaning of renunciation, is not even aware of that problem, never resigns itself; resignation is for beaten people, as beaten paths are for beaten men. Poor Lucienne, who thought that if only things had been different it might have worked. There are no objective conditions. Did I ever feel that a bright flame was smoldering beneath the ashes? Ah, la, la . . . it is in vain that I ask my soul, it is in vain that I probe its depths, I can detect no deep vibration. In the gray spaces within, there is nothing but ruins, beneath other ruins, beneath other ruins. But if there are ruins, perhaps there was once a temple, luminous columns, a flaming altar? It's only a thought.

Actually, there was never anything else, no doubt, but chaos.

Jacques Dupont was the only one left. For thirteen years we had been seated at the same table across from each other, doing our work: lists, lists, lists. For the week or two it would take the boss to find someone to replace me, Jacques would have to do double work. But wasn't the new employee already hired by the boss? And besides, Dupont will have to get used to somebody else, to get annoyed and disgusted by the habits of the new employee, and then he will have to assimilate them—I refer to the habits—or pay no attention to them. He'll miss me. I'll have to come to see him from time to time. Wait for him at the exit, perhaps. To have a drink together, as we did in the past, which already seems to him like the good old days. And I shall give him my address, right, he will come and visit me.

"Of course," I say to him, "of course."

"Unless, now that you're rich . . ."

"Don't be silly, don't be silly. I won't forget you. How could I forget you? One never forgets anything, neither the good nor the bad, especially someone like you who . . ."

In short, in a word, he stayed and joined me for lunch at the café. We offered the café owner a drink. Then it was his turn to offer us one.

"You will come and see us, Monsieur? One doesn't forget friends as easily as all that. Fifteen years now you've been eating here. I've taken good care of you. Oh, I know, there are restaurants on every corner, cafés too, but no one will ever take as good care of you as I have. Now what would you like to order?"

Jacques and I were seated at the table by the window. It was a gray day. We ordered some paté, sardines, boeuf bourguignon, coffee, and two bottles of Beaujolais. We asked for more coffee, several coffees, several more coffees laced with cognac, then he left. Then I left.

I was in a hurry to move. For years I had been living in a small room in a small hotel. In winter my room was warm enough. In summer, too warm. I had a bed with a red bedspread, a closet, a chair, a table, a washbasin; the toilet was down the hall. Since there were several rooms on my floor, all with tenants, we often had to stand in line to use the toilet. Frequently there were quarrels. I was obliged to get up very early to arrive there first, even if it meant going back to bed later on for three-quarters of an hour, for I had to be at work at 8:30. If you weren't in by 8:45, they marked you absent for the day. When you didn't sign your card, you had to pay a penalty. My room was on the sixth floor, the top floor, with slightly sloping ceilings. It had a little square balcony surrounded by an iron railing. It was a bright room. In one corner I had about twenty books. I would have liked to have more, but I had no book-cases or any shelves. Books that I read I would throw away. I had kept Dostoevski's *The Possessed, The Wretched* by Victor Hugo, *The Three Musketeers, The Count of Monte-Cristo,* a volume of stories and tales by Kafka, Arsène Lupin, and a book by Rouletabille. On Sundays, I went to the movies. By myself. I no longer had any girl friends, and I was too shy to go up to a woman in the street, the way

Jacques Dupont did, his theory being that the street was the best place to make a pickup. Perhaps he was bragging. After the movies, I used to take a short stroll through the streets. I would window shop, vaguely eyeing this or that piece of merchandise, eyeing less vaguely the women passing by. Sometimes I went to a second movie, usually a detective story, or else I would take up station on the terrace of some café where I would drink beer after beer after beer.

I was more than a trifle bored. We all know that nothing is sadder than Sunday afternoon. Young couples—the pregnant mother pushing the baby carriage while the young father walks beside holding another youngster by the hand —made me feel like killing them. Or killing myself. But after the third or fourth beer, the whole thing became funny, and even happy. By the time night fell, the families out for a stroll were replaced by people or silhouettes that were less depressing. After two more beers, I attained a measure of happiness. I no longer felt my body. I smiled blissfully. I returned to my little hotel, opened the door of my room, and stumbled inside. I had a lot of trouble getting undressed. I piled my clothes as best I could on the chair and fell into bed. As a precaution, I put my alarm clock on the bed table, but always, or almost always, I awoke a few moments before it went off. The ring of the alarm clock terrified even my subconscious, which is what made me wake up just before the alarm was due to ring. I would turn on the light and remain in bed for a few minutes more, awake or having drifted back to sleep. The reason I would get drunk on Sunday was to forget that I had to begin another week on Monday morning. Monday mornings, my head bursting, my tongue thick, were times of desolation and despair. For me, to wash, shave, and brush my teeth on Monday was a task that seemed to me even more impossible than it was on other mornings. A mountain. As painful a prison as all the other days, but different from the Sunday prison. I didn't live too far from the office. I went downstairs and out into the street, which was filled with people, all in a hurry, like me returning to their daily hells. At the corner café I stopped for a few seconds for a strong coffee and a quick drink. Afterward I felt better, or more neutral. It was usually on Mondays that I arrived late at the office and found my time card, which I was supposed to sign, already gone, removed from its slot.

"How was your Sunday?" Jacques asked me. "Did you have a good time?"

"I had so much fun my stomach still hurts from laughing."

Jacques was married. It bored him to go to the movies with his wife. He would have preferred to go alone, or with somebody else. I was bored to go to the movies alone. But once I was settled in front of the screen, I forgot myself. I would have been hard pressed to tell anyone the plot of the film, or the films, that I had seen. I was there watching the images move; I saw people chasing one another, fighting, and killing one another with a great deal of sound and fury, usually with guns. Jacques didn't go to just any old film; he was fussy. He was cultured. He went on at great length about the pictures he had seen. But I knew that he had been just as bored as I. Without admitting it to himself. Monday is the most painful day of the week, the hardest to get through. You still had the whole week ahead of you, and I bore it on my back as Atlas bore the world. On Monday evening I freed myself of one-sixth of my weekly weight. It went on that way day after day, gradually growing lighter throughout the week. By Friday evening I was, as it were, happy. There was still Saturday morning to get through, but we had Saturday afternoons free. Then I would pay myself a good, hearty meal. I spent Saturday afternoon stretched out on my bed. But with the advent of Saturday evening, the anxiety began, for now there was only Sunday between me and painful Monday. If Monday was the heaviest and the most loaded day of the week, Sunday was the emptiest.

Well, I had no one to blame but myself. I could have pursued my studies. My father died when I was five. It was my mother who supported me. I don't know why she had broken off relations with her family. Because of my father, I think, whom she had married against her family's wishes. My father had been dead now for a long time, but she still hadn't made up with her family. She worked hard, poor dear, she too had an office, but that didn't make ends meet. In the evening, when she came home, she addressed envelopes. I helped her for a little while, then she would send me off to do my homework. I used to fall asleep over my books and notebooks. It made my mother sad that I was a dunce. "Work," she would say to me. "Later on you can make up your mind if you don't want to work, but now you should buckle down, darling, and I know you will, won't you? You'll be a teacher, an engineer, a doctor. You'll be someone important. You'll have lots of people working under you."

I would have liked to work, just to please her; it really

hurt her deeply to see that I was doing badly in my studies. She took care of me as best she could, complaining not about her own fate but about mine: "You could have been an ambassador," she would say to me, "and worn a cutaway. You could have been a famous writer and won all sorts of literary prizes. Or a general, with rows and rows of ribbons. But it takes hard work. I can tell you, people who have worked hard have made it, and you're no dumber than most of them. Come on! Buckle down! . . . " All I brought back from school were poor marks. She killed herself for me. I was drafted into the army. As soon as I got out, my mother found me this job, with the help of her boss, the man for whom she addressed envelopes, who was a friend of the other boss who was about to become mine. "You still have time," she said to me, "you still have plenty of time to finish school. You can study in the evening." I'd been working for only a few weeks in my office when my mother died suddenly, of a cerebral hemorrhage. She had done her duty, she had supported me, she had found me a boss, and helped me land a job—kind of a job.

I was overcome with remorse and impotence. Remorse because I realized that her life had been twice a failure: first because of my father, and second because I hadn't lived up to her expectations, I hadn't helped her, because I hadn't been able to help her make a success of her second life. I didn't want to go on living in the dark apartment, with two rooms and a kitchen, where I had seen her suffer through so many painful years. That was why I decided to move to a modest hotel, which wasn't exactly what you would call cheerful, either. And so it was I found myself sitting across from Jacques Dupont, who for hours on end would tell me the same jokes, over and over. Every evening after work, while I was wandering from café to café, Jacques was studying and learning. He read novels and ideological works. He joined a revolutionary party. Each evening he would learn the various doctrines and policies of the party, which doubtless he absorbed in his sleep, and the following morning he would launch an all-out attack on society. And since I was the only person to whom he talked he looked daggers at me and shook his forefinger at me threateningly. The upshot was that he gave me such a bad conscience I felt responsible for all the ills engendered by "the system." It was I who was the society ridden with ills, the evil system, the scapegoat. In all fairness, I have to admit that it didn't go on for very long, an hour at the most, for the boss, or his secretary, who from their office nearby had heard fragments of the speech, would charge out, come over to our table, and demand that we go back to work. Thus calm would be restored, and at noon Jacques and I would go out together for a friendly apéritif at the usual café. In the afternoon he would be too tired to go on with his diatribes; not only that, we had to work twice as fast to make up for the time we had lost in the morning because of Jacques' speeches. As we left the office, Jacques and I both noticed that in the fall each day was a little shorter than the day before. Starting in January, sometimes he, sometimes I, would remark that each succeeding day was one minute longer than the day before.

I wasn't a rebel. Which is not to imply that I was re-signed, for the fact was I didn't know what I ought to resign myself to, or what society I should contemplate in order to live a happy life. I was neither sad nor happy; I was there, from head to foot caught up in the cosmogony which could never be any different from what it was, and no society of any kind could ever change that situation one iota. It was given once and for all, with its nights and its days, its sun and its stars, the earth and water, and any change in what was given us was more than the imagination could grasp. Above, there was the sky; the earth supported my feet; there were laws of gravity and other laws to which the whole cosmic order submitted, and as for us, we were part and parcel of the same. Still, once or twice I did revolt. Sometimes, following a business lunch, the stockholders or the board of directors would come to inspect the offices. They gave us twenty-four hours' advance notice. We swept, we cleaned, we shaved until our faces literally shone, we put on smocks that had been freshly laundered and ironed, and then we waited for these gentlemen. Our boss leading the way, they entered our offices. We stood up to receive them. They didn't say hello to us, nor did they respond to our greetings; they didn't even see us. They examined the files and records, and listened to the boss's explanations. Many of them had hats on their heads. Others wore no hat at all. But all six or seven of them looked flushed, as a result of the copious meal that they had just eaten. And each wore a red ribbon stretched across his chest, or the rosette of the Legion of Honor.

As soon as the door had closed behind them, Jacques Dupont started to scream: "And to think that we're the ones who feed them! They grow fat off us, profit from the fruits of our labor. We sweat, and they prosper!"

The phrasing of Jacques Dupont's declaration struck me

as a trifle excessive, in that neither he nor I sweated when we worked, both of us being fairly comfortably seated. Therefore my own anger didn't last very long. They're not long for this world, I said to myself, just look at how red their faces are. Apoplexy will soon do them in. And who are we anyway, Jacques Dupont and I? Two men, two miserable insects among three billion others. The shareholders numbered six or seven, but still among the three billion other members of the human race. Replace them? With what, and with whom? Whether society changed or not, I was among those whom it dragged along with it no matter which way it went.

And yet I felt uncomfortable, ill at ease. Not knowing which way to turn so that I wouldn't feel it, or so that I would feel it as little as possible. From time to time, especially during adolescence, I had been troubled by the mystery of the universe. The notion of an infinite universe is beyond our ability to comprehend. And yet at school I had been told time and again in all kinds of classes that, indeed, the universe was infinite. And then I'd been told the universe was finite, not infinite, which seemed to me even less conceivable, if that is possible, for what was out there "beyond"? I suspect that the universe is neither finite nor infinite, the words finite and infinite being expressions which ultimately are meaningless. If one cannot conceive of either the finite or the infinite, the non-finite or non-infinite, which are so basic and simple, which we should have been able to conceive of, what could we do but not think about them? The full spectrum of our reason crumbles into chaos. What can we know of justice, of the physical order, of history, of the laws of nature, of the world, if the very bases of our possible comprehension are unknown even by ourselves? The best thing is not to think about it. Let's think of nothing. Let's judge nothing. Otherwise I'll go stark raving mad. But what is a madman? Another question better left unasked. And so it was that for years I was able to live in the here and now, a moment in time without shareholders, an indefinite moment. And yet that moment did have a history, since there had been Lucienne, Juliette, and Jeanine. Since there had been periods of time, weekends and the beginnings of weeks. And what was more, an organism that I began to feel as something heavy, unpleasant, something which was me and not me. In spite of myself, in spite of my simple, very basic philosophy, boredom and malaise had infected me, had entered my being and overwhelmed my defenses, despite all my efforts, despite my shield of non-thought. Arriving at work every day was no longer a habit, it was a constraint. I couldn't explain it to myself. Nothing is explainable. But I endured. And above all, no longer to see Jacques Dupont or Pierre Ramboule or the boss was in itself a kind of happiness. To leave, to free myself. Here, in the midst of total incomprehension, were a few little things which could be understood. Even if we were incapable of understanding the universe or defining its great laws, at least we could maneuver within a tiny universe, within the great infinity, or the non-finite non-infinity.

It was early in October. The weather was still lovely and warm. I started to look for an apartment. At first I thought about living on a major thoroughfare with lots of trees. Or rather, overlooking a park, on les Buttes Chaumont, for example. And then I said to myself that I would be better off living in Versailles, in the vicinity of the park. But there was nothing in Versailles except for official buildings, or apartment buildings far too expensive for my budget. The fact was, I could not throw money out the window. I had in mind to live for a long time on my income. The problem was: with inflation rampant, would my capital last me long enough? I would have to invest it. They advised me to buy some stocks, or bonds. I understood nothing about stocks or bonds and had little or no confidence in either. What if I were to invest my money in a company in competition with my former boss? The manager of the little hotel where I lived wanted to renovate the place. He didn't want it to be a hotel for lower-echelon employees any more, tenants who paid little and late, the kind of employee I had been up till now—though, fortunately, now I no longer was. I couldn't buy a farm; I didn't know how to plant and till the fields, I had never spent more than forty-eight hours in the country. The hotel manager's offer tempted me for a while. Actually, he wanted to turn the hotel into a whorehouse. And then I said to myself that I'd have too many problems with the police and the underworld. The manager assured me that he had friends in both camps. I didn't find that very reassuring. I decided that the best thing for me was not to get involved with businessmen. During the day I looked for a place to live, and at night I tossed and turned in my bed, unable to sleep, thinking of the money that had fallen into my hands like manna from heaven, money I wanted to make sure I didn't lose. At dawn, a phrase I had heard in I don't know what conversation a long time ago, before my inheritance, came back to me: "I'm going to put my money into brick and mortar." Of course! Buy houses, and then rent them out. But rent them to whom? To people who wouldn't pay, or pay only a little at a time, who would dirty everything and, once the lease was signed, prevent me from raising my rents at least in proportion to the cost of living?

In spite of all these concerns, in the morning when I left my hotel I went joyfully down the stairs, whistling all the while, and emerged into the street at ten or eleven, whenever I wanted. It was fun, I felt happy, and then I realized that it wasn't all that much fun and that I wasn't all that happy. Had a weight been lifted from my back? The weight of living? I had been born bowed down with grief. The universe seemed to me a kind of enormous cage, or rather a big prison, with the sky a ceiling, and the horizon walls beyond which there had to be something else. But what? I was in a vast space, and yet it was locked. Or rather, I had the feeling I was in a huge ship, and the sky above was an enormous cover. There was a crowd of prisoners, and as far as I could tell most of them were unaware of their condition. What was there beyond the walls? Well, when you really thought about it, there was a positive side to the picture: the daily prison, the little jail inside the big one, had opened its doors to me. Now I was able to stroll at will along the main thoroughfares, the broad avenues of the big jail. It was a world comparable to a zoo in which the animals enjoyed a kind of semi-freedom, with man-made mountains, artificial woods, and imitation lakes, but at the far reaches there were still the same old fences.

And yet I still had not solved the apartment problem. I went looking for something in buildings still under construction. But to see walls being erected made me sick. Walls being built are reminiscent more of prison walls than are the old walls of old houses. One has the impression that the walls of old houses are slightly used and that, as time goes by, one will be able to see through them into the great outdoors. Even if this outdoors is ultimately another, vaster indoors. As far as business matters were concerned, I had finally found a solution. I divided my capital into three equal parts, which I gave to three lawyers, each of whom promised to give me a seven percent return on my capital. They loaned the money to various people in the construction business. When the borrowers paid off the full amount, the lawyers found other people to lend the money to. For me, that was the best solution, for the lawyers confirmed a conclusion I had already reached myself, namely that to invest in stocks or bonds in these times of financial uncertainty and universal economic distress was most unwise. In the end I found a place to live. An apartment which in no way reminded me of the sad, musty little apartment where I had lived with my mother, or, of course, the hotel room.

It was an apartment located in the near suburbs. On the fourth floor of a building that was neither very old nor very new, a solidly constructed building dating from 1865. The entrance was dark. On the left as you went into the apartment was the toilet. A few feet farther on, also on the left, was the door to the kitchen. The walls were rather dirty, but a coat of paint would take care of that. On the right, a glass door opened into a large room illuminated by three windows, with the result that the room was not only large but light. After the kitchen, the hallway turned to the left and led to a bathroom and to two other rooms, both of which looked onto the courtyard. I decided that one of them would be my bedroom. What could I use the other one for? I would use it for a storeroom; I would put my suitcases there, my clothes; it would be a closet. The large room was a corner room, two of whose windows overlooked an avenue, while the third faced a small street filled with private homes, surrounded by small yards or gardens. Huge trucks and buses rumbled along the avenue, making the house shake ever so slightly. The noise didn't bother me. The bus stop was directly across from the two windows, on the far sidewalk. Within a stone's throw from where I lived was everything I needed. A few steps from my building was a bar-restaurant where I could eat my meals. Two doors farther along, a laundromat. Next to the bus stop there was a tobacconist who also sold magazines and newspapers, and next to him was a store that sold radios and electrical appliances. But when I looked out the other window, the one overlooking the narrow street, I had the impression I was far away, in some little provincial town. I immediately realized the advantage to be derived from that double view. In the space of ten feet I could travel from the city to the country. I decided to move in as soon as possible. The person who was selling me the apartment was an old lady whose husband had recently died. She was filled with projects for the future. She was going to live with an unmarried niece, who worked as a cashier in some business or other. The niece had two small rooms, which ought to suffice for both of them. The niece wanted to retire. With her modest pension, and the money that the old lady would add to it, they could both live reasonably comfortably for a fairly long time. For ten years, perhaps, or even fifteen, by pinching their pennies. The old lady would not live more than fifteen years. And the niece, with the money she would realize from selling her little apartment on the Riviera to rich Americans, would be able to end her days in a home for the elderly, where she would be well cared for.

A few hundred yards from my new home there was a furniture store. Fortunately the store owner did not deal in antiques; the furniture that he sold was shiny and new. Not everything he had for sale was in his shop, of course. But anything that caught one's eye could be brought in from the main store. All of it was good, solid merchandise fashioned by skilled, honest artisans. In my first room I installed a big, bright yellow sideboard, which I placed against the right wall. The style of the sideboard was hard to pinpoint. About 1925, the man at the store told me, slightly modified to imitate a more ancient model. "It was one of our own designers," he told me, "a designer from our main store who built it." For the middle of the room I bought a round table large enough for six, but it had extra leaves so that when it was fully open it could actually seat ten. I would never have that many people to dinner. But you never know; perhaps I would make up with my cousins, my mother's nieces and nephews. Perhaps I would meet people in the neighborhood. Perhaps I would even have a busy social life. I ordered ten chairs, just as yellow and solid. Six of them I put around the table. The other four I put against the wall, two between the windows that faced the avenue, and the other two next to the glass door. The only rug I bought was a round, pinkish-red rug to go under the dining-room table. But I liked my comfort, too. For the living-room part of the room, I ordered two easy chairs and had them moved in. I put a blue easy chair facing one of the windows overlooking the avenue, the farthest one. Next to the window which looked out onto the narrow street I put a sofa, also blue. It was on this sofa that I planned to stretch out to read the paper. From the ceiling I had a chandelier hung. Next to the sofa I placed a floor lamp with an orange lampshade. Curtains in the windows —red curtains with a green-leaf pattern—heavy, double curtains that gave an impression of comfort and wealth. Next to the sideboard I put a clock. I had the floor waxed, because I like well-waxed floors. There was a time when I thought of putting in fluorescent lighting, but I was advised against it. The only place there would be neon was in the kitchen. This living room-dining room, with its spanking new furniture, looked beautiful indeed. I had an all-new kitchen installed, too. In the bedroom, I put a king-size bed, large enough to sleep two or three. I prefer to have plenty of room in bed, for I toss and turn a lot. I bought a wardrobe and a valet stand. Near the window, a small easy chair upholstered with a flower pattern, and curtains matching the easy chair and the bedspread, green and red.

In the local hardware store, I bought knives, forks and spoons; plates and cups of the same pattern, with roses on them. I also bought a breakfast set for two. The spoons were silver, the cups had a gold rim. I put the set on a Chinese tray and put it on the sideboard. I'll only use it on Sundays, I thought.

I bought sheets and pillowcases. And I bought a new, ready-to-wear suit for holidays: a good-looking gray suit with a square print pattern. I left my dirty clothes back at the hotel, taking with me only a brown suitcoat and a pair of black velvet trousers. Among my books, I took *The Wretched* by Victor Hugo, *The Three Musketeers* by Alexander Dumas, and as an afterthought, two other books: *Twenty Years Later* and *The Viscount of Bragelonne*.

I still didn't leave the hotel; I had to wait till I had found a maid to keep house for me. I hadn't the faintest idea how to use a broom, much less a vacuum cleaner. The last days I spent in the hotel were filled with joy and yet at the same time tinged with regret. A whole life: Jeanine, Juliette, and Lucienne; the short walk I had to take each day from the hotel to the office; the old café: all that was dead and gone. Life is beautiful: a whole existence of old papers and office dust; the bed in my hotel room which often remained unmade from morn till night when I came home from the office, because of the dearth of hired help, the only maid being an aged hunchback who did the best she could. The rude awakenings in the morning; the mad rush to the office in the hope of still finding my time card; the joy at reaching the office on time so that I could sign it; the anger and frustration on those mornings when I reached the office thirty seconds after the card had been taken away—all that seemed to me to be enveloped in a kind of happiness that I had not previously noted, as all of a sudden I found a kind of beauty in the dust, the crowded street, the mass of people hurrying like me to work, the hundreds and hundreds of gray faces, faces which were but clouds doubtless concealing the sun that we all bear within us, if only we knew it. The past is always tender and beautiful, something to be looked upon with sorrow, whose qualities we notice only when they are gone. We need a certain perspective, and that goes for pen-pushers and statesmen alike, millionaires or tramps. It's true, it's true: we all contain within ourselves a world full of sunshine, a world in which joy is constantly ready and waiting to unfurl, if only we realized it, I mean if only we realized it in time. How lovely ugliness is, how happy sadness, and boredom is due only to our ignorance! The iciest cold cannot resist the warmth of the human heart. Assuming one knows which button to push in order to light it. In short, we look back nostalgically on everything, which proves without question that it was beautiful.

Actually, this succession of euphoric ideas occurred to me at the local café, after several drinks. I had to stop. Not drink too much, for if you do the opposite vision takes over, draping everything in various shades of gray, cloaking every thought in anguish and distress until you regret having lived for naught in this vale of woe. Alcohol can be a blessing, but a precarious one, to say the least. A blessing, or the path to understanding? When do I hit upon the truth, when I see everything as desolation and despair, or when I see all creation as a joyous month of May in full bloom? But we cannot know, our ignorance is boundless. We have neither the right to judge, nor the possibility of judging. It's a question of having confidence. The question is: in whom?

I realized that I thought too much, I who have promised myself not to think at all, which is much the wiser course since, in any case, no one understands a word I say.

I philosophize too much. That's my weakness. If I had been less of a philosopher I would have had a happier life. When one is not a great philosopher, one should not philosophize. And even when they are great they are pessimistic, or their conclusions are impossible to fathom. Or else they suggest that we should give free rein to our slightest desire, and where would that lead us? At least a good half of the world's population suffers from desires either exacerbated or frustrated. If they gave free rein to their desires, let out all their pent-up frustrations, they would all go around killing one another, or perhaps committing suicide en masse; but whether they tried to kill one another or commit suicide they would inevitably be further frustrated, for the police would step in and stop them. Unless the police decided it would be better to join them than fight them, unless the police also decided to give free rein to their slightest desires, that solution would prove impossible, except during revolutionary periods when everyone kills everything, all the while proclaiming that they are doing what they are doing so that people can live, live better. Revolution leads to tyranny, it brings it on posthaste, and then the most violent desires are quickly repressed. But there are many people, perhaps a majority of the population, who do not want to give free rein to their desires because they don't want to admit that they have any such desires, or because they aren't strong enough, or because they just don't have any desires at all. I don't have any desires, or rather only a few, or rather I don't have them any more. If I have any, they're not worth being exploited and encouraged. Perhaps I actually do have desires. But they're dormant. I'm not inclined to wake them up. What are my desires? That people leave me alone; that other people's desires leave me alone and don't involve me in their repercussions. What I desire most of all is not to have any desires. And yet I notice that I do have some. All right, the desire for women is gone. Forever, I hope. Besides, the level of my desires in that area were very low. That's what saved me from women. But I still have a lingering desire to drink wine, which is what awakens, or rather keeps alive, however slightly, my desire for living. Otherwise everything would by now be extinguished, and I would already be dead.

I've often told myself that my depression stemmed from the newspapers. From one end of the planet to the other there is nothing but mass killings, rebellions, crimes of passion, earthquakes, fires, anarchies, and tyrannies. When all is said and done, I spend most of my time down in the dumps. Perhaps it's because I read too many newspapers. I won't read them any more. We have the great good fortune to be living on the last remaining segment on the planet which is not yet in flames. Let's take advantage of it. "Aren't you ashamed to have no goal in life, to be living for nothing?" Pierre Ramboule asked me one day, unless it was Jacques, I don't remember which. After a thorough self-examination, I came to the conclusion that I wasn't ashamed: is it better to encourage others to massacre one another, or to let them live and die as best they can? I don't feel obliged to answer that question.

The maid in my hotel had a sister who was also a hunchback, she told me, but younger than she, who wasn't afraid to work because, aside from her hump, she was in relatively good health. She made careful note of my new address, not far from the Porte de Châtillon.

I took my last suitcase. I bid a final farewell to the *patron* of the hotel. I called a taxi. I looked out at the street, at the people pouring out of their offices, for it was lunchtime. Many of my former colleagues used to eat their noon meals in the canteen that my ex-boss had established in collaboration with several other small businesses in the area. I used to eat there too on occasion. They had a very good potato-and-herring salad. A fine rain was falling. I climbed into the taxi.

It took us forever to drive across Paris. What a mob! Bumper-to-bumper traffic as far as the eye could see, and yet it was the time of day when most people should have been eating their lunch. From the gare du Nord to the avenue de Châtillon was, admittedly, a considerable distance. One street followed another in seemingly endless succession; they were all the same. So were the people. Tens of thousands of people, all of whom looked alike: they were walking straight ahead as though they had some clearly defined goal in mind. It was as though the streets were peopled with dogs. Dogs are the only ones who run about like that, as though they knew exactly where they're going. On the pont Saint-Michel, it stopped raining. At the rue des Écoles, the clouds parted and the sun came out. But everywhere, everywhere, all the people looked the same. It was like one or two people being multiplied ad infinitum. It was ten past one when I reached my new home. I went into the building, carrying my suitcase, and said hello to the concierges, an elderly couple, living on a pension. He was tall, fat, and red; she was smaller, with white hair, and a distrustful, shrewish air, needless to say. She thinks she's really a concierge. I had already seen her during my earlier visits, before I had bought the apartment. She played her concierge role to the hilt, to such a degree she made it hard to believe she was anything else—a woman, for instance.

She said to me: "Your maid's already here, Monsieur. I gave her the key. She's upstairs in the apartment."

"Yes, I told her to go on up."

It wasn't hard to climb the stairs with my suitcase. The suitcase wasn't very heavy.

"My husband can give you a hand . . ."

"That won't be necessary. I can handle it myself."

"Are you sure you don't want anyone to help you with your suitcase?" the concierge insisted.

My apartment was on the fourth floor, the door to the left. I rang the doorbell. Jeanne, the maid, opened the door. Beyond the dark entrance hallway was the living room. It was very bright; there wasn't a cloud in the sky, and above the roofs of the houses that lined the street that had a provincial-town look about it, the sky was one long stretch of uninterrupted blue. Two old ladies were chatting on their doorsteps. Farther along to the right, two men, who also looked as though they were retired, were standing on the sidewalk, also talking. From the other window, the one overlooking the avenue de Châtillon, it was crowded sidewalks, lots of noise, buses. Once again I was struck by the difference between the peace of the provincial side street and the clamor of the avenue.

"You know, I've been working like a dog," Jeanne said to me.

"I can see," I replied, "the floor is beautifully waxed. We'll have to be careful not to slip and fall. But I like a well-waxed floor. And the sideboard there, it's so clean and sparkling. Thank you, Jeanne."

She helped me off with my coat, which she hung on the rack in the hallway.

"You'll have to change the place of the hat rack, Monsieur," she said. "It's too near the kitchen. Your coat will smell of grease. I bought some meat at the butcher's, a veal cutlet. Would you like me to cook it for you?"

"No," I said, "I think I'll save it for tomorrow. You're coming tomorrow, aren't you? To make the bed, and make sure the whole house is spick-and-span. I like clean sheets, too. And if there's anything I hate it's dirty dishes."

"Yes," she replied, "the fact is, the hotel you've been living in can't have been very clean."

"That's why I want to change. Don't worry about unpacking the suitcase. That can wait till tomorrow."

I was hungry, and couldn't wait to try out the little restaurant on the corner.

I walked down the three flights of stairs, my hand on the railing, looking at the threadbare carpet. I would have been hard pressed to say what the original color might have been. On the ground floor I made a point of smiling at the concierge, to which she responded by what I can only describe as a gnashing of her teeth, a rictus I found difficult to interpret. I was not yet in her good graces; it takes a while before they adopt you. I pushed open the glass door leading to the hallway, crossed the hallway to the wide-open outside door, exited, turned left into the quiet street, then left again and, after a few more steps, found myself in a sea of sound. At the bus stop, people were waiting for the bus; most of them probably went home for lunch; then they would have to take another bus back to work. For a few seconds, a big truck hid them from view. They reappeared, the bus arrived, they rushed headlong into it. Not far from where I was standing, a few hundred yards away, there was some business, with offices. I congratulated myself on not having to take a bus any more, not having to rush through lunch in order to dash back to the office. I didn't have an office any more. I pushed open the door of the little restaurant. Almost all the tables were occupied, by workers, white-collar employees who seemed less rushed than their colleagues since, not having a two-way bus trip to contend with, they gained a little time. Someone got up and left his table; it was a tiny table for one, or at the very most two, in the corner by the window. I went over and sat down at that table. I sat with my back to the room; I don't much enjoy seeing other people eat. I preferred to face the window. The waitress cleared the table of the plate and silverware of the man who had preceded me. She left, then returned and replaced the wine-stained paper tablecloth with a new one; then she gave me a fresh plate and clean silverware. I placed my order: filet of herring with potatoes, with olive oil dressing; boeuf bourguignon; camembert cheese; a half-bottle of Beaujolais. "No," I said, "on second thought make it a full bottle. If I don't drink it all, you can save the rest for me tomorrow, since I plan to eat here every day."

Outside the traffic was heavy, a steady stream. Yellow cars, black cars, red cars went by; a few taxis; dark-clad pedestrians, or was it only their mood that was dark? Girls, office workers dressed in very short, brightly colored dresses with flower patterns, the cheerfulness of which contrasted sharply with their faces, which seemed sad or preoccupied, probably at the thought of having to go back to work. Or perhaps they had other worries. The day was rather dark. It wasn't raining.

I think that was the first time I ever really looked at the daily spectacle of that street. I found it most interesting. Fascinating, in fact. An amazing number of people in that passing parade, so many different faces and so many identical thoughts. Or almost identical. My boy friend; my girl friend; where shall I spend my vacation this year, for vacation time will soon be here? The kid on the way we hadn't planned for; the children already born we've had to put in a day-care center, since we both work. Those two elderly people who are still working. That other old man, already retired, living out his remaining days as best he could with the meager pension he had been given, thinking about death, which wasn't all that far off, which was already stretching out its arms to take him. How strange it all is. And that's the way it's been for centuries. And then the school children, the teachers and professors. In other parts of town, in other streets, the wealthy. But I'm wealthy, too, I reminded myself happily. A wealthy man in a poor-man's part of town. I might have chosen to live in a better part of town, in the posh park district, for instance, in any one of several buildings with broad staircases and polite concierges. I was on the one hand torn between a feeling of sadness and dejection, a certain weariness, a sense of disgust and, on the other hand, my amazement at seeing all these people, some with vehicles, some without, racing, running, rushing to and fro, in a scene of perpetual motion. Movement, movement: how strange it all was! My daydream, or what passed for it, was interrupted by the arrival of my herring and potato salad, with olive oil dressing. They brought me the Beaujolais; I poured myself a glass. Before I had a chance to raise it to my mouth, a cloud parted and sunshine poured in on my white paper tablecloth, my plate, my herring, and my bottle. I downed the glass in one gulp, and it was as though the sun had also entered me. There was still a measure of joy possible, if you stood aside and simply watched the madding crowd. I was still young; I could still look forward to my fair share of sunny days. I turned around and looked at all the people at their tables. They were others in another light. I turned back to my plate and concentrated on my salad. As usual, I had come to have lunch, by sheer force of habit, without really being hungry. And now, suddenly, I was hungry, because of the sun. I wolfed down the boeuf bourguignon, then the cheese, downed the entire bottle of wine, and drank a useless coffee, for I'm not a coffee drinker. That is why, after my coffee, I ordered a chocolate cake smothered in whipped cream. I sat there at my table, watching all those people in the street as though it were the first time I had ever seen such a sight. I felt good. Excellent, in fact. I found the idea of leaving the restaurant distasteful, but I knew I had to, I was the last person still there. With great reluctance, I got up, said good-bye to the owners as I passed, and found myself back out in the street. But then the thought that I could continue watching from my apartment window, seated or stretched out on my sofa, which was right next to it, immediately cheered me. I turned the corner into the narrow, provincial street, was again greeted by the sight of the little houses with their tiny gardens, again had the impression that I had made a long trip in the space of a few seconds, and entered my building. The concierge half-opened her curtains, saw me, and closed the curtains. I started up the stairs. On the third floor, I saw a lady who was taking a little dog out for a walk. When it saw me the dog started barking.

"Fido, behave yourself!" said the lady to the dog. Then she said to me, "I beg your pardon, he barks whenever he sees someone he doesn't know. Later on, he'll get used to you."

"Don't give it another thought, Madame, not another thought."

I climbed another flight of stairs, and rang my doorbell: no answer. That meant that Jeanne had left. I took the key from my pocket, opened the door, and went inside. A little light filtered through from the living room. I went into the sun-drenched room. She had really done a good job: the whole place was spanking clean. The sideboard, the table, the floor. And then I suddenly remembered that I had not bought the afternoon paper. Once again I went out into the hallway, locked my door, walked down the three flights. From behind her curtains, the concierge watched me go by. I walked to the corner, turned left, then left again; the tobacconist who sold papers was on the opposite side of the avenue. I waited for a moment, then when the cars and two motorcycles stopped at the red light, I crossed the street, bought my paper, turned back the way I had come, and waited till the cars coming in the opposite direction had stopped. Next I crossed the avenue, turned right, then, a few steps farther on, right again. I walked for a while. I went into my building. Again the concierge peeked through her curtains at me. I turned and looked back at her. When she saw that I saw that she was looking at me, she closed her curtains. I climbed the first flight of stairs. I felt like having a nip on my sofa. I had forgotten to tell Jeanne to buy me a bottle of brandy. Should I go back downstairs? I stood there for a few seconds trying to make up my mind. Then I decided to retrace my steps. I walked back down the one flight and turned toward the concierge's glass door, hoping she wouldn't see me. Again she half-opened her curtains, then she closed them much more quickly than before, so that they continued to rustle for a few seconds.

I walked through the lobby, emerged into the street, turned left, walked a few steps, then left again, passed the restaurant, left it behind. At the corner there was a liquor store. Luckily for me, it wasn't closed. I bought a bottle of brandy, then retraced my steps, again passing the little restaurant, turned right, then, at the corner, which I reached without incident, I turned and went into my building, trying to look as dignified as possible, while at the same time doing my best to conceal the bottle. All I saw was the concierge's eye in the crack of her curtains. Again I climbed the stairs to the second floor, paused for a moment on the landing to catch my breath, then climbed the next flight of stairs, paused for a slightly longer time, again to catch my breath. Then, with my hand on the railing, I began the ascent to the fourth floor. I reached my landing, headed for my door, which was on the left, reached into my pocket for my key: it wasn't there. I had a moment of panic. I looked for it in my left pocket. There it was. I remembered having put it there. I put the bottle of brandy down on the doormat, opened the door, then locked it behind me. Then I remembered the bottle on the doormat. I unlocked the door, picked up the bottle, then locked the door again. I had met no one on the stairs during my climb. They must all have been at work. I went into the living room. Near the sofa, I put down the bottle and the paper, then went out into the hallway to take off my hat and coat. Came back, took a glass from the sideboard, closed the sideboard door, and, having skirted the table, headed for the sofa. I stretched out on the sofa near the window. Got up to take off my shoes, stretched out again on the blue sofa. I raised myself on one elbow to pour some brandy into the glass I had brought from the sideboard; I recorked the bottle, downed the glass in two gulps, took my newspaper and once again stretched out. The back of the sofa was raised; I gazed at my green shoes. On page one the headlines announced a disastrous plane crash. Somewhere in the middle of the Pacific a plane had disappeared with a hundred and twenty-five passengers on board, and seven crew members. I studied the photographs of the two stewardesses. The quality was poor. From the photos it was impossible to tell whether they had been pretty. They must have been, though, from the vital statistics that were provided. One was five foot seven, and the other five foot five. They had both been blondes. It was one of the worst air disasters ever. There hadn't been one as important for a long time. I pictured the stewardess, the one who was five foot five. Five foot seven was perhaps too tall for a girl. Perhaps she had looked like Lucienne. She must have had pretty legs, and looked pert and smart in her navy-blue uniform and hostess's cap. Had her eyes been blue or black? Probably blue, since she had been English, not American. I had only taken a plane twice in my life: once to go to Marseille. On my way back I had taken the train, for the plane trip had made me nervous. The second time was when I went to Nice to see a great aunt who was dying. That time I had been less nervous and enjoyed the flight more. It had been a beautiful trip, with blue sky all around, above the bank of clouds. But I didn't take the plane back that time, either. I had come back with three friends in a car: a couple, both quinquagenarians and their son of twenty-five who was studying medicine. I should have, and even could have, taken much longer trips. Now I really should travel, since I had money: to Japan, to South America. I'll go, I told myself. First I'll take it easy for a while, for a few months, perhaps for a year, and after that I may start a whole other life, a life of pleasure and adventure. But not right now. Now I still wasn't up to all those long and complicated errands: telephoning the travel agents, going down to their offices, filling out forms to obtain a passport. Buying myself clothes suitable for traveling. Fine clothes. But later. From my sofa I could see the blue sky; that's what gave me the itch to fly. And yet I would be hard pressed to say that I was uncomfortable on the sofa. I picked up my newspaper again: another child kidnapped, and war raging more or less throughout the world. What an egotist, I thought to myself. I felt so happy that I didn't have to make it, I mean war. How lucky I was, not to have any children to worry about, either. For the time being, for the time being how fortunate I was not going to work. No one can force me to go to the office. I drank a second glass of brandy; I looked up at the sky; I got up and went over to gaze down at all the people milling about on the avenue; then, going to the other window, I looked out at the peaceful street with its little houses. I drank a third glass, recorked the bottle and put it back in the sideboard. I took a little stroll, several times around the table. The light, the brandy, the freedom: all buoyed me, filled me with a kind of happiness. What if I went out? What if I went down to the office and waited around for my ex-colleagues? Oh, I was fine right here where I was. I had all the time in the world. I stretched out again on the sofa. Remained in that position for a few moments. Every so often I would open my eyes, then shut them again; it was a dreamless dream. I drifted off.

Then I got to my feet. I left the living room and walked down the long hallway to take a closer look at the bedroom. The wallpaper was very well done, and very pretty: roses against a white background. I'm very fond of flowers. Unless it was the paperhanger who liked them. But in any event I was all for having flowers on the bed, the easy chair, the walls. It starts your day off right to wake up and see flowers all around. It doesn't remind you of the country, but it did remind me of a certain garden from my childhood where a friend of my parents, who loved gardening, had planted a wide variety of flowers. But that I would see tomorrow when I opened my eyes. I came back out into the dark hallway, which was very long. On my right as I emerged from the bedroom was the bathroom. I went into it and stayed there for exactly two seconds.

This is my bathroom, I said to myself. No more need to

stand in line the way I used to at the hotel, with the whole floor making a mad dash for the toilet.

I also liked this dark hallway; the darkness lent it an air of mystery. It was a place you could walk in. Walk to one end, retrace your steps, walk to the other end, repeat the process; it reminded me of some underground passageway, or one of those secret hallways through which courtesans had to walk in order to reach the bed chamber of the lord. Back in the living room, I looked down again at the avenue, then at the little street. I couldn't make up my mind. If I hurried, I could still make it to my old office in time to catch a few of my former co-workers as they were leaving. I thought about it for a second, then said to myself that I still had plenty of things to discover in my new neighborhood, within striking distance of the house. All I had visited so far was the avenue and the narrow little street. I still hadn't explored the streets on the far side of the block of houses. At this time of year, early autumn, it was still light out.

No, no, I won't go back to the office.

I looked out the window. The blue sky was not quite the same as when I had last looked. The sun, itself less bright than before, made the blue less radiant. It was when the sun made the sky seem less bright that I became aware that the sky was a roof. The earth is a globe inside another globe which in all likelihood is inside another globe which itself is inside another globe which . . . Whenever I tried to picture the finitude of a globe in the finitude of another globe in the finitude of another globe in the finitude of another globe in the finitude of another globe—all these finitudes being infinitely linked one to the other—I felt nauseous, got a terrible headache. Felt dizzy. I found it inadmissible that we are powerless to conceive of the universe, to understand the "how" of things; that is, what makes them tick. Not to mention that as we all know the shape of things is but the image we make of them. . . . Since I was twelve I have periodically been plagued by that question, which always gave me the same, horrible feeling of frustration and nausea. What do all those people do who are walking down there to and fro, presumably to some destination, or running to catch their buses? If everyone began to think such thoughts or imagine the unimaginable, they would stop dead in their tracks. I had already said to myself: don't think, since we can't think. People tend to avoid or forget the unthinkable; their thinking begins where the unthinkable ends; they base their thinking on the unthinkable, and for me that too is unthinkable. And yet, they have invented arithmetic, geometry, algebra . . . but algebra also leads you right back to the edge of the abyss. They have built machines, organized societies, and yet they turn their backs on the absolute question, the question without an answer.

Perhaps it's foolish pride, trying to ponder what ought not to be pondered. But there is no such thing as pride; what is pride? The fact remains I can't get started. I think that I'm at the wall of the world; forget the other side of the wall. I can't make up my mind to move away from the foot of the wall. Perhaps it's a sickness. I'm all alone here, at the foot of that wall. All alone, like a fool. They—I refer to the others—have made all kinds of progress; they organize societies which, admittedly, sometimes work and sometimes don't. And there are some wild machines. Personally, all I do is look at the wall, my back to the world. I've already suggested to myself, yes, I have, to *not* think, since one can't think. How strange: they think that the world, the universe, that creation, that the whole kit and caboodle is perfectly natural and normal, admitted facts. And they're the scholars, the learned ones, while I'm the dunce, the ignoramus. We're in jail, of course, in jail. It's because I want to know everything that I know nothing. Is it possible they'll succeed in giving the answer? In a few dozen, a few hundred generations, they will conceive of the inconceivable, they may be able to imagine the unimaginable. If they don't stop working, if they still take buses, publish books, compute and reckon, set off to conquer the stars, if microscopes discover that there is an infinitely small universe, it must be because they feel, subconsciously and naturally, that they will succeed. But as for me, I have the feeling that they are building on a void—and that too is only a word. We give meaningless names to things about which we have nothing meaningful to say, to nothings about which we can say nothing. The infinitely small . . . Obsessed by the infinitely large, I allowed myself to become also obsessed by the infinitely small. . . .

These are the kinds of stupid questions that kept me from getting ahead, that kept me from enjoying the pleasant things in life. Oh, but that's just not true! There are some things, a few things, which I do enjoy. But I couldn't bear that anxiety any more—the angst, is it? I couldn't bear any longer what I called the nausea of the finitude and the nausea of the infinite. Everyone's gone through that phase, at thirteen, at fifteen, at eighteen. And it's not that they went beyond it because, in fact, they were dealing with the limitless, but rather they stopped taking it into account. Or they stopped worrying about it, or else they simply forgot it. There are some people who never even asked themselves the question. Politicians, for instance. Politicians are either there or here, or totally at home. Their finitude is more than sufficient unto itself. I don't mean to imply that I'm any better than they, which does not mean that they are any better than I. Which doesn't mean anything at all. Yes, for me that doesn't mean anything at all. Absolute values don't exist. In this globe, which is a globe caught in a globe which is in a globe which is in a globe. It's enough to make your head spin again. I headed toward the sideboard. I opened the door and took out the bottle of brandy. One after the other, I gulped down five glasses. Lord, was that good! All the questions became blunted and blurred around the edges, and I felt warm and happy. No, not happy so much as freed from all these questions. I was no longer the prisoner of the globe alone, but also of that warm blanket of alcohol which envelops you. But the nausea was gone. I was no longer thinking the unthinkable. Not gone, perhaps, but leaving. Perhaps it's a kind of curse, always looking at the wall. For the time being, the curse has been lifted. How I wish it were always like that! What I wouldn't have given to be like everyone else! I was filled with a desire to stretch out on the sofa, but I knew if I did I would fall asleep till the following morning. No, I had to go out. To the restaurant.

On my way to the restaurant, I went the other way around, which gave me a chance to see two other streets in the neighborhood. So there was that provincial street with the little houses, two or three of which looked like chalets, then I turned right. It was a depressing street, because of the rundown houses right next to houses that were too spanking clean, four-story buildings subsidized by the government. Several motorcyclists were standing around, revving up their cycles, getting ready to roar away together, doubtless emulating some American film they had just seen, which gave them a taste for terrorizing. There must have been five or six of them in all, each holding his cycle with one hand, grouped around one motorcycle that apparently had some engine trouble. They were obviously having a ball with it, gunning it full blast. The noise was deafening. Two or three of the other cycles blasted in succession, and I wasted little time putting as much space as possible between me and those horrible cycles and that dreadful noise whose aggressive intentions, fully realized, I felt in every painful pore of my body. Three or four workers in overalls were wending their way homeward, not without having stopped to bend an elbow or two in the local bistros, to judge by their trail. I felt very middle-class. And wretched at feeling middle-class, as though I had committed some sin. Which one? In vain I kept telling myself over and over what I already knew, namely that there is no sin, no blame, but my reason made no headway against my irrationality. Incredible, those opposition people and papers! Incredible the strength of the clichés that you reject but which, in some insidious way, make their way past your defenses and permeate your being! No one is to blame for anything. No one is guilty of anything. Or else everyone is guilty of everything, which comes to the same thing. But how weak and vulnerable are those who feel guilty, even though they think they aren't. What a schism between reason and unreason! Those who feel and at the same time believe themselves guilty might just as well stop struggling and give up. Do themselves in. What is to prevent them now from killing themselves? Whereas I, the muddle-headed and confused . . .

At the corner, I turned right and found myself in a broader thoroughfare, a street almost as wide as the avenue. Parallel to the provincial street where the retired people lived, this street wasn't exactly the height of gaiety either. Very few dwellings, but a great many enormous workshops or depots. The buildings that constituted the back of the factory were on the left side of the street. Workers were leaving the factory area. Not even a bar. A garage, the one that housed the buses that drove up and down the avenue where the restaurant was located. In marked contrast to the rest of the scene, there was a girl dressed in pink. There were a few trees, their leaves still intact, but covered with dust. In the morning, and again in the evening, when the workers arrived and departed, there was a fair amount of traffic on the street, big trucks first and foremost, and a goodly number of workers riding their bicycles. It was coming up to dusk. I walked another hundred yards or so until I reached the corner, then I turned right. It was my avenue, the one I could see from my window; it was as though I already knew it, as though I had already seen it and trod it for months, even for years. Admittedly, I had come here before to buy the apartment, but it was only since this morning, when I had really looked at it, that I knew it. Lost in the crowd, I headed toward the restaurant. Across the street, the same sort of people I had noted earlier were still standing in line for the bus. I opened the restaurant door and cast a worried glance at the corner table, to see if it was free. I was relieved to see it was. It was going to be my table. The restaurant was already fairly crowded, and the lights were on. I made my way among the tables to my corner, placed my hat on the hat rack, and sat down. Outside, the street lights went on, too. The waitress came over to my table and said:

"Weren't you here at lunch?"

"Yes. I'll be eating here every day. Can you save me the same table?"

She answered that that was hardly the custom in a restaurant of that category. Only in the larger restaurants could one reserve a table. But she said she would try, provided I would eat fairly early. I told her that I was a man of regular habits and that I could be there promptly at twelve-thirty for lunch, for example, and in the evening at seven sharp.

"I can see that you're a creature of habit, all right," she told me. But I must have struck her as a pretty strange fellow. She handed me the menu. At noon, I had already had the herring and potato salad, with olive oil dressing, and since I wanted a change I asked her for a sardine appetizer to start with. For my main course, a steak, with spaghetti on the side. A *baba au rhum* for dessert. And, of course, a bottle of Beaujolais.

"I see you like your food," the waitress said.

"True," I answered, "I like my food, and from what I've seen it's good here. And I also like your Beaujolais."

"The owner knows a wine grower who ships it to him directly. And besides, everything is fresh and clean here. Look at the other customers. They look happy and have

hearty appetites. This is the best restaurant in the neighborhood. There's a brasserie down the block, but it's always
empty. And another restaurant they call 'auberge,' trying
to be chic."

I learned she was the owner's sister-in-law. His wife's
sister. One of her cousins also worked in the place, tending
bar. It was the owner himself who did the buying and
carted the food back from the market.

"It's better to keep it in the family," she said. "You get
along better that way. But I must be going. I'll bring you
your order right away."

I turned to the window. It's fun to watch the people
going by. I prefer daylight. Dusk fills me with all sorts of
apprehension. But to see people passing by, all kinds of
people, soothes you, gives you courage. When I was a little
boy I was afraid of the dark. In those days my mother
used to take me out shopping with her. She held me by the
hand. It was a crowded street, not unlike this one, though
narrower. Naturally she knew lots of people in the neighborhood. She used to stop and exchange a few words with
one lady, gossip a bit with another, chew the fat with one
of the tradesmen. I remember that swarming crowd which,
despite the semi-obscurity, for the street was poorly lighted,
filled me with a comfortable feeling. Most of these silhouettes, these people, no longer exist. I was remembering
a street of ghosts. And suddenly the present passers-by outside my window seemed to me to be ghosts, too. Nothing
but ghosts. I felt my heart constrict, and again anxiety
overwhelmed me. I was afraid. Of nothing. Of everything.
Fortunately, the wine and the sardines arrived. "Here you
are," the waitress said. She took the trouble to pour the

wine herself. Then she left. I drank that glass, and poured myself a second. Things began to look better. Something approximating a feeling of joy. I often have a momentary movement in the direction of joy, a leap toward happiness, but the energy is lacking, and these fits and starts, if they are the terms, fall back, short of the mark. I used to have a method for bringing myself out of my moments of depression or fear. It didn't always work. In any case, it consisted of looking with great intensity at the people and objects around me. Staring at them. Looking at them as long and hard as I could, and then suddenly it was as though I were seeing everything and everyone for the first time. And then it all became incomprehensible and strange.

I made a concerted effort, trying to forget all the paths that I had seen, and all the towns and cities and all the streets and all the people and all the things. I had been cast out into the world, and I was becoming aware of it as though for the first time. I wanted to rediscover that strangeness about the world that I sometimes manage to obtain. It's as though you were witnessing a show of some kind, that is, as though I were in the background, at a certain distance from the events taking place, as though I were not involved, were no longer that actor or that supernumerary that I am, that we habitually are, out of habit. In the world but not of the world. Sometimes it only increased my anxiety, but most of the time it had the opposite effect, chasing it quite away. No more involuntary and categoric judgment, for each time it seems to us that this universal machine, and these people and these streets and these movements, are ugly or beautiful, good or bad, favorable or unfavorable, dangerous or reassuring. I managed to reach a kind of moral neutrality. Or an aesthetic neutrality. "They" were no longer my brothers; I made a conscious effort not to understand the words the people in the restaurant were saying. That way, their words turned into noise, or sounded like some language you didn't understand. It all became, was nothing more than, fleeting apparitions, a kind of illusion of the void. The others went by in the street, in a kind of street, a kind of space, for the first and last time. I was the only one who really existed. The rest was blurred. Again I was in front of the inconceivable wall. Where are we? Where was I? Oh, yes, the plates, the knives and forks, and the buses and the passers-by are things, or something, you don't know what to do with any more, something you can't use any more! I was the only one alive. As the others passed by and disappeared, I felt unique in this welter which couldn't be real. The real was becoming a kind of empty space that I was filling. A euphoric expansion of the self, myself, and the more it seemed to me that "all the rest" scarcely existed, the more I was sure I really did exist. But I had to restrain that euphoria; not destroy it, but really restrain it. Otherwise I would take on such dimensions that by occupying the entire space that one might refer to as existential, I would again find myself hard against the invisible walls of the inconceivable. I don't know whether I'm saying exactly what I mean. There's no way of describing this state in words. Perhaps I mean something else altogether, or something else in addition. A kind of reason kept telling me that I couldn't be the only one. "The others were 'me's,' just like me"; reason, which I tried to stifle, kept whispering to me.

It's when I feel myself alone, cosmically alone, as though I were my own creator, my own god, the master of apparitions, that I feel that I'm out of danger. Generally one isn't alone in one's solitude. People take the rest with them. They are isolated, but isolation isn't absolute solitude, which is cosmic; the other kind, the little solitude, is only social. In absolute solitude there is nothing else. What tortures you are the memories, the images, the presence of others. Tortures and disturbs. There is one solitude which is both boring and unbearable, and that is the one where you compare yourself to others, call on them, have need of them, a solitude in which you flee from them because you believe in their existence. Since you're afraid of others, you rush forward as though to disarm them. But I wasn't God, and it wasn't me concocting all these fleeting apparitions, all this pretense and show; "they" were offering it to me, "they" were introducing me to it. Ah, this "they." And yet it was indeed that, I refer to the "they," that was behind it all. I submitted; I tried not to submit, I tried to keep out of it, off to one side, merely looking on, but I was obliged to take it into consideration.

Still in all, I was not yet reintegrated, I was not completely sucked up by existence, by that kind of universe; I was still outside for a few moments. The voices were still indistinct murmurs and the people were ghosts. And then the fall. All of a sudden, normality once again became normal; I was inside. Things assumed their former identities. I made yet another effort to revert to the other state, the one without a name. I stared as hard as I could at a red wine stain on the paper tablecloth. I had already tried that experiment and made it work before. It was all a question of looking at something until you no longer remember what it was. It was supposed not to be a wine stain any longer, it was supposed to become something, I don't know what, on that other thing, the tablecloth, which was no longer a tablecloth, nor a white space, nor the site of a stain. Thus I could extract not much, no, but nonetheless a little, from that space in something else indefinable but analogous to a space somewhere else. It also put me into the "somewhere else." Am I clear?

The trouble was, I couldn't concentrate. Perhaps because of the waitress, who called over in my direction as she passed by, "How come you're not eating your steak?" And yet when I'm well ensconced in the somewhere else, I take everything with me there, even the most innocuous phrases, not to mention the most pregnant, as I take people's gesticulation, which becomes something resembling gesticulation but no longer is. Often all I have to do is repeat over and over as fast as I can the word "horse," or the word "table," until the notion is drained of its contents and all meaning disappears. But no, tonight it wasn't working.

"But I am," I told the waitress. "In fact, you can even bring me my dessert. And a coffee later. No, bring it with the dessert." The voices, which had melted into a barely audible hum, had once again become hard and cruel.

Ah, yes, everything else was back in place: the lamps hanging from the ceiling weren't even moving; not even an earthquake. When I first attempted this kind of experiment, when I was fifteen or seventeen, the somewhere else came more quickly. Most of the time, it was shrouded in a luminous light. And when the other world receded, for a long time, for days on end, I had a clear memory of a luminous world. I was convinced that it had really existed, that it still did exist somewhere, and that I could find it again. It was a joyful memory, one that stayed with me for days, perhaps even for weeks. Now, when the advent of that other world has become increasingly difficult, and ever more rare, its disappearance leaves me unnerved, distraught, and in a state akin to depression. I'm not even sure any more that I really felt what I felt. I'm not sure any more it really happened. Everything had reverted to its former identity; everything could be referred to again by its name. I finished my meal, drank my coffee, and then what? There is an old saying that tells us we ought to enjoy whatever bounties life offers us, however middling they may be. For a long time I had lived in accordance with this principle. Then I had learned not to be too upset, either by the little things that life brings our way, or by the larger ones. It's no easy task, though, to put up with day-to-day existence; and yet, all things considered, idleness has to be preferable to work. If I have to choose between work and worry, I always chose, I always prefer worry, a certain kind of worry. Tonight I found it was difficult to leave the restaurant. I ordered a pear brandy. Aside from my own, there was only one other table still occupied, by a young couple, presumably in love, like so many millions of other young couples.

I was going to have to resign myself to leaving. I had already paid the bill. I took my hat from the hat rack. I bid the waitress good night, and could see that she was relieved to see me going, although she was perfectly friendly. She probably wanted to go to the movies or meet her boy friend and watch television. Say, that's what I'll do:

rent a TV set, to make my evenings less long, to help me fall asleep.

"Oh, Monsieur, I'm so tired I'm going home and fall asleep . . ." the waitress said to me. And yet she looked wide awake. I'll wager she doesn't go to bed just to *sleep*. She told me her name was Yvonne. But she was sorry, she didn't have time for small talk right now; no matter, there was always tomorrow, and the day after.

I left the restaurant and turned right. There were still a lot of people out on the well-lighted avenue. Fewer, though. At the corner I turned right into the narrow street, where there were only a few pedestrians. Not everyone was in bed, though; many windows were still lighted. I reached the door of my building. I went into the hallway. I walked past the concierge's door. I began to climb the stairs toward the second floor when the concierge's door opened and she appeared for a moment. I bid her good night. She retreated into her room without answering.

I'll give her tips and presents so she'll like me and be all smiles, I said to myself as I replaced my hat on my head. Faces that eye me distrustfully, especially those that say nothing, displease me no end. At the office, little love had been lost among us, because of the boss, who was never pleased about anything and always played favorites, his choice depending on his mood, and because of the women who left you, who moved from one employee to another, with the result that we always lived on a shaky foundation of minor irritation and petty jealousies. But with all that it was, nonetheless, a life. What kind of life? Full of little surprises, little mishaps, reconciliations. I climbed the stairs toward the third floor. From behind the door of the apartment to the right, a dog barked. I climbed the stairs toward the fourth floor, arrived at my apartment, opened my door, closed it behind me. I pressed the button to turn on the light, put my hat on the hat rack. I turned on the light in the living room. I drew the curtains. I stretched out on the sofa. Then I got up. I sank down into my easy chair. Your own place. How nice it is to be in your own place. But is it really as nice as all that? Yes, it really is. There are countries where you have to be prepared for anything, the police for instance, who have the right to enter your home at any hour of the day or night. Nor did I have anything to fear from thieves. The neighborhood I had chosen, and the apartment, were modest enough to deter would-be thieves. But I had to find a few little things to do. Get to know the neighborhood better. Get to know the building. Should I strike up relations? I wasn't quite clear on that point. People can interfere with your habits. And then there was the problem of what you would say to them. I have nothing worthwhile to say to other people. And what others say doesn't interest me, either. The presence of other people has always bothered me. There was a kind of invisible partition between them and me. Not always. In fact, five or six faces were all I needed. In the next few days I would draw up the rules and regulations for my new life. The idea of pouring myself another smidgen of brandy crossed my mind. But I thought of the next morning, of the possible nausea, the hangover. We shall see what we shall see, I said to myself, we'll get things shipshape before long. It wasn't much, but it was something. Life is full of little surprises, all sorts of unexpected things can happen to you. Little things, not big things. I didn't like big adventures;

there's something disagreeable about them, fatiguing, and in the long run all they bring is trouble.

Only when I got to know the neighborhood better, and had explored all the nooks and crannies of my apartment, would I be in a state to see tiny changes, minor metamorphoses of light. I still wasn't well enough acquainted with my furniture, nor did I know how many flowers there were, or the quality of the colors. I got up and went over to where I kept my few books. I had read them all. There were several that I had read a long time ago. But as soon as you open one of them to the first page the whole story generally comes flooding back. Still, there were times when I enjoyed rereading the books. You discover that there are all sorts of details that were not firmly fixed in your memory. Such and such an event, or even a whole scene. I couldn't decide which to read, so chose none. I turned out the light in the living room, found myself in the hallway which I had already lighted, headed toward my bedroom, opened the door, lighted the lamp, turned out the hallway light, and began to undress.

This is the first time in my life that I'm sleeping in this room, in this big bed. I made up my mind not to forget this initial contact. Wasn't a new era about to dawn for me? No more alarm clocks, I said to myself. They really must envy me at the office. I turned out the light. I enjoy escaping into sleep. That phrase has often occurred to me, but I never really understood it very well: escaping from what? I'm the constant dreamer. I only dream of what happens to me in my daily life. Neutral dreams, gray-tinted, expressing neither desires nor horrors, it seems to me. Apparently we have deep-seated desires. There are people who can help explain them to you. I'd be curious to know. I've only had dreams of the sort that might be called "blue" two or three times in my life, as I recall. Dreams that you're sorry you can't remember, that you can't seize at dawn, when all you can touch are the fleeing shadows which disappear in the cruel light of day. And our entire life falls to pieces. If you don't want to suffer, you have to resign yourself. Resign yourself. I kept telling myself over and over to be resigned. Often I even manage to resign myself, or attain something approximating resignation. It isn't a profound, a real resignation. From time to time anger rears its ugly head. First it takes the form of a kind of discontent which grows inside me, invades me, embraces me. No, I shall never get over the loss, never shall I be able to forget that I have not been able to see over that wall which rises to the sky. How can one resign oneself to the ignorance in which, despite science, despite theology, despite the wisdom of the ages, we are steeped? I have learned nothing since I was born, and I know I shall never learn anything. What I would like to remove are the limits of the imagination. Blow up the walls of the imagination. But they will never crumble, and I shall die as ignorant as the day I was born. It's inconceivable not to be able to conceive of the inconceivable. All these technicians, all these politicians, these peasants and pedants, these artisans, all these rich and these poor can live so easily within the confines of these walls. It's not a matter of pride. I don't want to know any more about it than the others; I want us all to know. "It is unimaginable, therefore let us not imagine the unimaginable," wrote one philosopher, a few pages of whose work I read not long ago, standing in a bookstore perusing the uncut pages of the book. I have never recovered from my initial surprise at making contact with the world, a feeling of surprise and wonderment that cannot be dismissed. We are told to free ourselves from that feeling of astonishment and move on to other things. But in that case, on what basis can we found any knowledge or morality? There is no way that basis can be ignorance, and yet we are swimming in ignorance; our point of departure, our foundation, is nothing but the void. How can we build on nothing? We have a few practical applications at our disposal. I know that I can go from one place to another. I know that I can go to the restaurant. I know that restaurants have been constructed. I know there are motors. I know there is technical knowledge. It seems to me very strange that there is without question a technical know-how that makes sense, that works, based on nothing. That represents still another level of my astonishment. Who allows us that, or how is it allowed, how can it be? But once and for all, a limited knowledge is no knowledge at all. The whole universe and all the creatures therein are manipulated by instincts and reflections with which we have been endowed but which are valid only for a brief period. We are acted upon; we do not act. I think I'm eating for myself. Actually, I'm eating out of my instinct for self-preservation. I think that I love and that I'm making love for myself, but I am only obeying laws which control me, I am simply acting to perpetuate the species. "Laws" because I can find no other imaginable words to describe these things, these principles, that act upon me. We are sociologically conditioned, but that's nothing; biologically; even more than that: cosmically conditioned. And all those words I just said were said before I uttered them, planted within me. But this way of thinking and speaking—the terms I employ are approximate—does not interfere with reality, since I do not have a very clear idea what these words are, nor do I have a precise notion of reality, in fact no notion at all, nor even if reality is the expression of something, nor what that means.

I am trying to find the same solution again: stop thinking, if you can call that thinking, and if thought were really thought.

We submit. I submit. How pleased I am to submit. And there we are into resignation. And each time there is a little resignation in me, I feel relieved. Calm in a way, rested. I'm going to sleep. Be calm.

And then all of a sudden, unexpectedly as it always is when it leaps upon me, suddenly the idea that I'm going to die. I shouldn't be afraid of death, since I don't know what death is, and besides, haven't I said that I ought to give in and not fight it? To no avail. I jump out of bed, frightened out of my wits, I turn on the lights, run from one end of the room to the other, dash into the living room, turn on the lights there. When I lie down I can't lie still; the same when I sit or stand. So I move, I move, to and fro throughout the house; I light every light and I run, I run. Billions of people are subject to the same fears. Why are we acted upon in this way? Why? Reason goes out the window. Words meant to comfort fall on deaf ears. Fear oozes from my every pore. Like so many others, so many others, so many others. Each of the billions of people on the face of the earth is filled with such fear it's as though, in each person, he and billions of others were dying. Why was that? What caused it? Probably the fact that I had just moved to a new apartment, and my new freedom from the thousand little preoccupations of the office. I had not suffered an attack for a long time. I change my life, and in this new life I discover the same worries, the same fears that in my dull life of familiar routine had faded into the background. The old anxiety was back in full force, as strong and pervasive as when I first experienced my first astonishment in front of the wall of the world, and my first anxiety. No one is anything. And at the same time each of us is a whole universe. Let me lie down and cease to be, let me think no more, let me think no more. Then, at long last, fatigue overwhelmed me. A good and gentle fatigue, like a renunciation, came and took me just as the first rays of dawn began to probe the sky, and at last I could return to my bed, pull up the blankets, and doze off, then sink into a deeper sleep.

Each dawn is a beginning, or a new beginning. A resurrection. Death withdraws, slips away to hide from daylight. Morning as rebirth is not only a symbol. You can feel it, physically and psychologically. You can see it and hear it. When I was a little boy, already a worrywart, when my mother invited a couple of neighbors in to chat in the evening after work, they would sit in the room next to where my bed was and my mother would leave my door ajar. I must already have been afraid of the dark and the silence, for I can still remember how happy I was to hear, close beside me, the grown-ups talking, the reassuring murmur. I did my best to stay awake as long as possible, and then I would finally drift off, accompanied by that kind of concert. Now I like to lie in bed in the morning half asleep, listening to the morning noises, the neighbor's footsteps in the apartment upstairs, a window or door being opened, the radios playing; aware, too, of the morning smell of coffee. What I enjoy even more is the first rumble of the subway; or, in my new home, the sound of the first bus. But the rumble of the subway, which I shall hear no more here in the suburbs, that underground rumble which made the walls vibrate ever so slightly, that muffled sound soothed and comforted me, and I would fall into a deep sleep. Then, alas, the shrill ring of the alarm clock would suddenly intrude. But here that would be gone. Aside from the noise of the alarm clock, noises in general don't bother me. The sounds of a hammer, an air hammer, of cars, saws, machines, I tame them, that is I don't try not to hear them, not to get angry at them, not to fight them. I listen to them carefully. In that way, a landscape of sounds builds up, interesting and auditory, like a score of *musique concrete*.

I was awakened by the doorbell. It was eleven o'clock. It was Jeanne, my cleaning lady. She apologized for being late, for she was due to arrive at ten, but she had a lot of work, and besides, her husband wasn't feeling well. But she didn't overdo her apologies, for she soon saw that I had just awakened and that her tardiness had allowed me to sleep an extra hour. I told her to begin in the living room, and I went into the bathroom. Not exactly a solarium, that bathroom. It looked out onto the courtyard of the building. But then, it wasn't exactly a coalbin, either. Still, I had to turn on the light. What a bore, these morning ablutions!

I always try to postpone them as long as I can. On Sundays, when I had no office to go to, I used to put them off till around two o'clock in the afternoon, when it was time to head for the restaurant, and even then I avoided shaving. But on weekdays I had no choice but to perform them earlier. Now, every day would be Sunday. I was afraid of turning into a bum. It was a real danger. This sluggishness, this morning idleness filled me with distress. Now, I realized, my sloth threatened to ruin my whole day. I told myself that I would have to ask Jeanne to come earlier, say at eight o'clock—no, let's not carry things too far—all right, nine, so that I would be obliged to wash and shave and dress at a reasonably early hour. I washed and shaved as fast as I could. With a kind of happiness. I said to myself, I'm going out, I'm going to see the street, the people, my whole new neighborhood. I could already picture the daylight streets filled with people. One day I would also have to take a stroll down the narrow street where the retired people lived. Get out into the world. Look at people with a mixture of interest and detachment. It was a pleasant prospect. I had all sorts of reasons to be happy. Why not profit from everything your eyes can see, everything your ears can hear? To be surrounded by all that, and at the same time outside. A spectator on the stage surrounded by actors. Anything at all can be fascinating and thrilling, dramatic, strange, unusual, mysterious: let your gaze follow the trail of a dog as he hurries along toward some goal or other. People who hurry toward some goal or other. Watch the people who are watching. Everything is a show, a spectacle dreamed up by . . . by whom? By God, let's admit it. Let's admit that I believe in that. But creation is like a big show, actually, even if it's one whose ins and outs, not to mention its ups and downs, I fail to understand. In any case, it's wild, that no one can deny. Maybe He allowed the world to make itself, without any outside help. Maybe I'm wrong once in a while. Maybe it isn't true that He conditions us in everything we do. Oh, yes, all you have to do is lift a corner of the frail curtain that covers the world with the banal and the ordinary which are within us rather than without, and you will see, if you look closely, that nothing is banal, all is both tragic and comic. I'm spouting nonsense, something else, something entirely different. The show that men put on, their theater, is only a poor substitute for the great theater.

It was already too late for breakfast. No matter, I'd go to the café and have a drink before lunch. It was almost noon; I could stay at the café, outside if the weather was good, inside if it wasn't, reading my paper. I left the key with Jeanne, reminding her to leave it under the mat. I had a feeling that she was vaguely upset to see me leave so soon. She wanted to chat. I had already remarked the day before that she had a tendency to go on at great length about her life. I didn't tell her anything at all about mine. She would have liked me to. But I had no intention of doing so: it was a secret between me and me. Why a secret? I asked myself. It's not a secret, and it's not a non-secret. It's only that it bores me to indulge in idle chatter. I left the apartment. Went down the stairs with a song in my heart, whistling the song, for two and a half stories. Then I stopped. I had to think of the concierge. Look dignified and respectable. I descended the last few steps calmly, almost solemnly. The concierge, sure enough, was at her post, the curtain raised a notch or two. Then she cracked open the door and looked out at me sternly. I made a pledge to myself that in the future I would walk on tiptoe. I greeted her timidly, which infuriated me, for I said to myself that, when all was said and done, she was my employee and I wasn't doing anything wrong. Hmm, this time I could have sworn I saw her smile. A trace of a smile. Maybe not. In any case, she didn't frown. It bothered me to think that I would have to walk past her door every day, confront her silent judgment; contempt would be closer to the mark. I was making it all up. I went outside, turned left, passed an old man in the little provincial street, walked a few steps down the avenue, then crossed and walked as far as the bus stop, behind which was the main entrance to the town hall. A few yards farther along, I turned right, walked parallel to the town hall, or rather parallel to the side wall of the town hall, until I reached the door through which the employees entered and from which they exited. I turned my back to that door, and crossed the street to the little café. A newsstand happened to be there. I bought a paper and sat down on the café terrace, which was covered, at a tiny round table next to the bay window. I ordered and drank a campari, then a second, then a third, then a seventh. I did my best not to order another. Perhaps because of the waiter, whom I was bothering too often and who looked as though he were sneering at me behind my back. Even more, he looked irritated. Maybe I was imagining things. Anyway, seven camparis was plenty. The slight happiness that I had felt that morning—only intermittently it is true, because of Jeanne who had filled my ears with her small talk and then because of the several-seconds-long stage fright I'd felt as I passed the concierge's door without escaping her evil eye—grew by leaps and bounds, stifling all anxiety, giving birth to quietude. I felt like laughing, a rather foolish laugh perhaps. Rather foolish? What difference did it make? I cast a quick glance at the news, both domestic and international and learned—the word is hardly appropriate, since I had long been aware of it—that on the home front people were not getting along. The discontent of the peasants was increasing, as was that of the workers, not to mention the dissatisfaction being expressed by members of middle management, artisans, and businessmen. One sensed as well that the police had had about all they could take, and were threatening to occupy the ministries. The intellectuals were angry beyond words. The students were too, because they did not want to work, or rather because there was no work for them, the economic situation being such that the number of jobs available for them was abysmally small, or would be once they had completed their difficult, boring, useless studies, or rather studies so interesting and indispensable to the progress of humanity that the students thought they ought to be paid a lot more. In other words, they would not enjoy the station in life which they had every right to expect in that society which, when all was said and done, was worthless. On this point, I was of the same opinion, though my reasons were different: society cannot be based on any morality or religion; the existential condition of man in itself, whether socially or extra-socially, is inadmissible. I never read philosophical articles to their conclusion. I put down my paper for a few moments and watched the crowd flowing by without really seeing it, for I was thinking, suddenly, that it wasn't true that we are conditioned, and acted upon. But who might this person be who is acted upon? Or those persons? What is this "I"? Does it exist? Yes, it does. But is it? Only if we believe in a soul cast into the world and submitting to it. All we are, perhaps, is knots, ephemeral intersections of energies, forces, various and contradictory tendencies which only death unties. And yet these forces, these energetic events are ourselves; we are built, we are produced, we are acted upon, but also we make ourselves, we act and we act upon ourselves. Oh, if only I had some philosophical talent! All the things I'd understand! I'd understand the same things I know now, but I would explain them to myself better, and I'd also be able to explain it better to others and exchange ideas. I also could have been a mathematician. A student mathematician, one of Lucienne's cousins, once told me that through mathematics you can prove the existence of God. Another mathematician told me that mathematics and physics were based on postulates and axioms which themselves were founded on the void. And yet that, I mean everything I see, has a structure. You can start from any postulates and axioms and you can build on them. There is nothing real. There is nothing false, nothing true, and yet the whole thing works, everything can be verified, one thing builds on another. God grants us that freedom, that there are whims and desires, interpretations and hypotheses which, while they may or may not contradict each other, are equally valid as bases for constructing this world or that. I heard a student, speaking to another student who did not agree with him—all this took place several years ago when I used to lunch at a restaurant not far from the office, and listen—I heard one or the other main-

tain that if the Nazis had won the war, their racial, biological, and economic theories would have proved true and
thus served as the basis for a culture just as solid as a
Marxist economic and biological vision. The most varied
and conflicting mathematical theories, and all kinds of
geometry, every geometry that has ever existed, do not
impede, but on the contrary serve as a basis for architec-
ture. What serves as our basis and point of departure is our
purpose, our design, our hypothesis, the hypothesis being
no more than our deep-rooted desire, or the expression of
various ethnic or kindred groups. Everything is subject to
verification, and can be verified. You make what you want,
fit the product to the image. When I say you I mean you,
not me. As for me, I'm out of it.

After my seventh drink, I kept thinking that there was
nothing real or anything unreal, no truth and no lie. Every
philosophy, as every theology, is good or bad, depending on
your point of view. That made me laugh. I watched the
people passing by. They are all different. And they're all
the same. The empirical is all that really matters. Only the
empirical, nothing else. What does that mean? How clever
to philosophize without ever having learned to philosophize,
especially after seven apéritifs. I picked up my paper. I
never read the sports section. These teams that throw
themselves at each other tooth and nail clearly illustrate
the fact that it isn't the ball that matters. And when the
bigger teams known as nations go after each other in the
same way, or when social classes declare war on one another, it's not for economic reasons any more than it's for
patriotic reasons, any more than it's for reasons of freedom
and justice for all. No, it's because they need to make war,

because they *want* to fight. Don't misunderstand me: I'm not one of those polemologists, if that's what they're called, I mean one who philosophizes about the causes and meaning of war. And besides, whether people make war or not doesn't interest me in the least. I'm completely non-aggressive, well, almost, that's how I'm different from the others. But I confess that I gladly read the newspaper articles dealing with crime. I don't like criminals. Nor do I feel any pity for the victims, or ever so seldom. . . . Why do I enjoy reading those articles? Because they break up the day's monotony. The fact is, they're fascinating. I've never read an article about national or international politics to the very end. I mean the editorializing bores me stiff. I'm the commentator of events. I know that people like to make war and at the same time detest it; I know that people are pawns of other people; I know that there are times when people would love to love one another, but that most of the time they hate one another, in spite of themselves. They are bored without realizing it. Perhaps they aren't bored. Personally, I often am. I have vertigo, and I'm afraid of being bored. Not too long ago I went into a depression, perhaps subconsciously to be in fashion, because of boredom, or being boredom itself. Anyone who writes about boredom can't really be bored. Boredom produces one of three things: either it paralyzes you, impels you to commit acts of destruction, or else puts you into what can only be termed a catatonic state, that is one resembling death. It was unbearable. No one could help me. I couldn't latch onto anything. When I say "unbearable," I find that the word is far from the truth. It was deadly, yes. It was as though I were drowning in air. I found it impossible to open any window overlooking the street, the world, anyone. Suffocation. What else can I say? . . . For weeks and even months on end, when the effort of moving required an extraordinary effort and made me suffer as much as not moving. Intolerable, yes, that's the term. Absolutely intolerable. The food I ate was tasteless. A corpse who wasn't dead, a man alive who really wasn't. Alone, in an endless desert. Or, on the contrary, in a cell, surrounded by walls, very high walls, with up on top a pale, gray light, insufficient to read by. What did it matter to me what people were saying? Their indifferent or friendly or unpleasant words did not reach me, or if they did I repelled them, or fled from them. When I saw two or three people arguing I grew afraid, and if ever I saw people parading in serried ranks, in uniform or out, whether the crowd was calm, boisterous or, quite simply, the army itself, I fainted. May fate preserve me from any kind of crowd.

But I couldn't bear being alone, either. For days and days and days on end I walked from the door to the window, the window to the door, unable to stop the to and fro. It wasn't anguish; it was boredom, a material boredom, a physical boredom which kept me from moving even as it prevented me from sitting down. Standing was equally impossible. Everything was painful, gangrene of the soul. I only hope it doesn't strike again. The seconds were long; no, endless. My only refuge was sleep. But unfortunately, I couldn't sleep all day long! And when I slept I dreamed that I was bored. In the past, in the old days, the boss was upset because they had given me a medical certificate. The doctor found he could do nothing for me; they had to take me to the clinic, pump me full of potent medicines, after which I could go back to work, I no longer had to go to the hospital. Boredom is worse than worry—in fact it's the opposite: when you're worried you're no longer bored. And so it was that I moved from boredom to worry, from worry to boredom. No, now I'm not worried any more, no, one shouldn't worry, but I sense that worry is lurking in the background, that it's watching me, a constant threat, that it can grow and envelop me, suffocate me. Oh, come now, the world is full of interesting things, chock full. All you have to do is look. There are people who only have to look at trees, to take a walk. They had advised me to take walks. Walks were more boring than boredom, sadder than sadness. So long as I don't fall back down into the yawning pit of boredom. Take a long and careful look at the world around you. Strip it of its "reality," do your best to rediscover its original wonder, not just in general but from moment to moment. Rediscover the feeling of the strange and exotic. Awake and see and feel what all that really is. Yes, existence, the world, people: all that is ghostly. All that actually matters is outside that, out beyond the wall. To be cast into the world is terrible, frightful. Come constantly back to the point of departure, keep from letting yourself go, keep from being caught. Standing with your back to the wall, view the world from that vantage point, or rather, turn around to face the wall, stand right next to it. Will it perhaps give way? How, as I stand with my back to the wall, can I explain that to myself, how can I watch the passing parade? You can't, not always. But it's the only way to escape boredom, total boredom. Let's not give it another thought. Let's think about something altogether different. There, I feel better. How good alcohol is!

I paid the bill, got up to leave, stumbled (but ever so slightly); it was twelve-thirty, I only hoped I wouldn't be late to the restaurant, that they would keep my table, I'm already used to it, I don't want any other. I emerged from the café, I crossed the street, a driver swore at me, I walked along the sidewalk until I came to the bus stop, directly in front of the main entrance to the town hall. I crossed the avenue, keeping to the crosswalk; a girl hit me with her elbow and said she was sorry; I poked a man with my elbow and said I was sorry. I found myself face to face with another man, not only face to face but nose to nose, unless the expression is eyeball to eyeball. I edged around him and reached the sidewalk on the other side, directly in front of the restaurant, my newspaper still under my arm. I opened the restaurant door, darted a look at my table, it was still free, in fact there was a little piece of cardboard perched on the tablecloth, which said "Reserved." I had already had too much to drink. What if I decided not to have anything to drink with lunch? Yvonne arrived, smiled and said hello, and asked if I wanted my bottle of Beaujolais. Whether out of timidity or temptation, I said yes. Mutton stew with potatoes was what she was recommending. She poured me a glass. I felt that she was looking at me with a kind of friendly concern. I downed the glass in a single gulp. The feeling of intoxication, of lightness, had disappeared, giving way to heaviness. But it wasn't all that unpleasant. I could no longer smell the mutton stew; I don't remember whether I had cheese or dessert, or both, but I clearly recall the coffee they served me: "Drink this. It's very strong. It'll wake you up."

It didn't wake me up. I can remember, but ever so

vaguely, that she led me to the door of the restaurant, then I hugged the walls to the right, and then I recall turning the corner and arriving at the front door of my building. I had a sudden surge of lucidity. Be careful not to zig or zag as you walk through the lobby, and stand up straight as you pass her door. She opened the door and gazed after me as I climbed the first few steps. I've forgotten the rest. All I remember is how hard it was to undress. The next day, I was awakened by Jeanne ringing the doorbell. She had come earlier, as I had asked her to. As soon as she entered the bedroom she gave me a funny look, just after she had said that she found I looked pretty funny. That headache, and that queasy feeling! There was only one remedy: a glass of brandy. No, two.

I splashed some water on my face and left the bathroom. Feeling slightly euphoric after my third glass, I drank a cup of strong coffee she had made for me and urged me to drink. Then I went and stretched out on the sofa, with the newspaper she had brought me. The father of a family had killed his wife and his son while they were sleeping. Axed them to death. A woman had killed her husband and daughter while they were sleeping. Shot them dead, with a revolver. Two lovers had committed suicide in a hotel room. A sexagenarian peasant had killed his neighbor, a quin-quagenarian poacher. His weapon had been a rifle. After a long search, the bloated body of a missing girl had been recovered from the river. A young man, either English or American, who was married to a Japanese girl, had committed hari-kari after she had left him for a German. A would-be suicide who had opened the gas jets in order to kill himself, had failed, but he had succeeded in blowing up the whole house, killing an elderly, retired couple and their grandson, all three crushed to death, whereas he, the would-be suicide, was dragged, still alive, from the ruins. War was also raging somewhere. In one battle, there had been 10,000 killed and 15,000 wounded. In the United States, a plane had exploded in mid-flight, while in Asia another had burst into flames as it had tried to land. Elsewhere, hostages had been seized. Still elsewhere, other hostages had been seized, but this time it was rightist terrorists who had done the kidnapping, while in the former instance the leftists were responsible. Revolts in Africa; having succeeded in obtaining their independence and freeing themselves from the colonial yoke, various tribes were killing one another the way they had done prior to colonization. Independence had given them the opportunity to revert to their good old tribal customs. Clearly, the whole situation was to be deplored. The world is going to perish for lack of oxygen. Some astronauts are on their way back from the moon. A new philosophy based on the notion of desire preaches the multiplication of carnivals. The Vatican counsels love and good will among men. One international association, with headquarters in Yokohama, Japan, asks that men kill one another in good spirits. That's interesting. But it seems, and I tend to believe the assumption correct, that it's all a big put-on. People don't kill one another as cheerfully as all that. To kill one another, a reasonable amount of anger and energy is indispensable. In some country halfway round the world, a million people have lost their lives since the beginning of the civil war. The opposing forces in the war are being aided in their struggle by three rival empires, all of whom are furnishing arms to one side or the other.

The Society for the Prevention of Cruelty to Animals is asking that people no longer kill baby seals. One young man kills his father because he was middle-class. In another country, where civil war is also raging, an entire village—men, women, children, even the elderly—is wiped out by its fellow citizens, because the religious sect to which the people of the village belonged forbade them from waging war, and therefore from choosing one side or the other.

Disappointing, all that. So bloody boring: every day the same thing. And yet, since people are all going to die sooner or later, what difference does it really make whether they are killed a trifle prematurely? And then you tell yourself: Come, come now, even though it's the same thing day in, day out, you have to admit it keeps you on your toes, the passing parade keeps your mind alert. I was about to drift off when Jeanne came into the living room.

As she rubbed the furniture to make it shine, she upbraided me, telling me that the life I led was unhealthy. She had remarked that I had a tendency to drink a little too much, it was bad for the health. Very bad, for a man at the height of his powers. Wasn't I going to buckle down and find some work for myself? All right, so I had an inheritance. That was no reason to sit around and do nothing all day. At least get married. Did I intend to go on living all alone, like some impotent? I ought to start a family. I should have children. Man is made to have children, and there's nothing cuter than little ones underfoot. And then when they grow up and you grow old, they don't abandon you to poverty; no, they reach out a helping hand when you need it most. If there's anything worse than living alone, it's dying alone, with no one around to offer you a little milk of human kindness. I didn't know what was in store for me. As for herself, she had a husband she didn't get along with too well, but now he was sick. They had had a child, a boy they had brought up with tender, loving care, he had a heart of gold, only he had gone away and left them; *he* had a heart of gold, it was only because of that wife of his. They hadn't heard from them in a long time. Apparently they had a baby. She had also had a daughter whom they had raised with similar loving care. A lovely girl. That is, she had been. But she too had had a baby, only the baby had died. After that she deserted her husband. She came back home for a while, then left again, she had begun living fast and loose, from all they had heard. Some cousins were in contact with her and kept them informed. Apparently she was on drugs. And yet he had no idea, all the love and care they had lavished on her! Children are ungrateful! You bleed yourself white for them, they aren't all that easy to bring up in the first place and then when they grow up they go away and leave you, forget you: the best thing is not to have any. Or if you do, make sure you have good children, not the ungrateful kind. As for the latter, you'd better not count on them to show you any gratitude in your time of need.

I told her I was sure she was right. That didn't stop her. She was still talking, with the dustrag in her right hand while she gesticulated with her left. She made me promise to marry and have children. I promised her that I fully intended to. She didn't seem convinced that I was telling her the truth. I swore that I was. Finally she left the room. It was still too early to go to the restaurant. What if I went for a walk first? It might prove fascinating. It might be fascinating, for instance, to discover a new café. There's no lack of bars and cafés, I might add. To have your apéritif in a different café every day, now that could be a real voyage of discovery. Trying a new drink every day would be, too. Yesterday, I had campari; today, it can be vermouth. I was suddenly overwhelmed with a buring desire to drink some vermouth in another café. I felt a wave of happiness rising irresistibly within me. I peered out the window to see if Jeanne was by chance still on the sidewalk, having a little chat with someone. If I saw her on my way out, or if she saw me, she might collar me and tell me Lord knows what. In fact, she might even introduce me to the other person and we'd end up having a three-way discussion.

She wasn't in the street. I dashed out of the apartment. She was downstairs, with the concierge, next to her door. When they saw me they stopped talking. Were they talking about me? All I want is for them to leave me alone. I can do whatever I want. I can loaf all day if I've a mind to. That's my business. Oh! I can feel myself getting angry. I hurried through the lobby. But before I exited I glanced back: I saw them looking at me. They were waiting till I had disappeared before going on with their backbiting, their malicious small talk. What could they be dreaming up about me? The whole concierge system is a kind of plot: if there had been no concierge, Jeanne would never have started sermonizing. Still, she's a good-hearted soul.

And yet there's no way around it, you have to take people into account. They do exist, since they bother me when they stick their noses into my business. That's all it takes for me to disconnect and sink back down among them. They draw you out of reality and enclose you in their own. You assume their point of view. You begin to see that you have to take other people into account. I can't take them into account, that goes without saying, but what I want to do above all is count on the somewhere else. It's the "elsewhere" that's true.

At the corner I turned left into the street and walked down it for a long time, two or three blocks—the day was dull and gray—before I came to a bistro at the corner of one street and the avenue which extended indefinitely, perhaps to the end of the world. I went into the bistro and ordered my drink; I downed my first, then my second vermouth. The bar itself was crowded with customers. Workers, both black and white, workers' helpers, a scattering of masons all bespattered with plaster, and then a tiny fellow in a light brown overcoat who was chatting with another seedy-looking fellow who towered over him. Both of them, this Mutt and Jeff pair, were going on like jaybirds, but in rather subdued tones. From their appearance, I assumed they were insurance salesmen. As for the others, the workers, they were talking much louder, slapping one another on the back now and then to emphasize a point. They called back and forth to one another from the opposite ends of the bar.

By slow degrees I was again caught up by that vision of the strangeness, the unusual aspect of the world. I realized, with all the acuity which is the hallmark of that intuition or state that, now that I had withdrawn into myself, these people were strangers to me. How difficult it is to see into the souls of others! And yet this time I would have liked to be closer to them. What would happen if I was closer to them, with them? How fascinating it would be! I would be alive. They were separated from me as though by a thick pane of unbreakable glass.

What could I do to get close to them? For me, these people, my fellowmen, were martians. The question was: were they behind the pane of glass like animals in a zoo, or was I? I carried my effort at separation even farther. By concentrating as hard as I could, I managed to make it appear that their movements, their gestures, struck me as helter-skelter, completely uncoordinated, a language I couldn't understand. Their words became increasingly garbled and confused. Shouts, inarticulate cries. Words stripped of any substance, like the bark minus the tree, or the rind without the fruit inside. Noise. They opened their mouths, they closed their mouths; they poured the contents of their glasses into their mouths, these gaping holes into which you put things which come out through other holes. I turned my head and looked out at the street. The façades of the building no longer looked like façades. The passersby no longer struck me as being passersby. Then I looked at my table, my glass, my hand. I moved my fingers; I felt like laughing. Then the terrible anxiety again. Then the feeling of incredible amazement. I looked around: what is all this? The question itself seemed meaningless to me. What does it mean to ask yourself what all this is? And what . . .

At the end, the far end of everything, I was. But nonetheless *there*, in the heart of things. Was it going to fall apart, be rent asunder, was I going to be able to see what was on the other side? What wasn't there? My eyes were not up to the task. I grasped my glass again in my hand, filled with fear, with hope. I felt it, though, I felt it. It woke me up. Or put me to sleep.

One day they came to install the telephone. I couldn't make up my mind whether to put it in the living room, next to the sofa for instance, or in the bedroom, on my night table. It might be pleasant to chat with people on the telephone (for it was my intention to renew old contacts, or make new ones), stretched out on the sofa, the daylight streaming in on me as I gazed out the window watching the people down below go by in the distance, that is in the street. I had lots to fill them in on since my departure, since I had last seen them. What had gone on at the office during these past four winter months? Some marriages, a few burials, a few new employees? I also had a real desire to see my old bistro again. That had been beautiful. Life is great when you take it as a whole, when you look back on it, on that kind of space that time turns into when everything has receded into the distance. It all becomes a single unit, a kind of house or château that you can visit room by room. How stupid of me not to have realized how beautiful it was. Soon, tomorrow, one of these days, I'll go out into the beauty of returning spring. Some leaves were already out on the trees. Life had seemed to me a burden; now it struck me as an ornament, a monument, a spectacle. To look at life from the viewpoint of someone already dead, if that were possible, is absolutely enchanting. Wonderful. And when you do, if you can, things appear so important, become so obviously meaningful! I felt nostalgic for the past. No matter. I can go back to the past whenever I want to. What ever became of Lucienne? I wondered if she had a child? And Juliette? And Jeanine? And the boss? Not such a bad sort when you look back. Merely stupid. And to think that I used to be frightened of his very shadow! He was rather comical, now that I think of it. Why is it that we always laugh too late? Nothing is really serious, since everything passes. Or rather recedes into the distance. And the past is shaped into a distinguishable whole, with well-defined contours, which the mind's eye can contain, examine closely, analyze, and reconstitute. When people do look back and realize how miraculous everything was, how sorry they must be not to have appreciated it at the time. That goes for the least little things: the smell of coffee in the morning, a funny quarrel—quarrels can be amusing— a fly in your soup, the dragoon's uniform, the dragoon *in* his uniform. Once they have retreated into the past everything, even the worst calamities—illnesses, epidemics, torture, war—don't hurt any more. They are curious phenomena, to be looked at and studied. Yes, I would call people, I would call everyone I knew.

I really shouldn't have the telephone installed in the living room. True, I want people to come and visit me, but I don't want them to bother me. I didn't want my number listed in the phone book, either. If some unwelcome or obtrusive people happened to knock on my door, they might see the telephone in the living room and ask me for my number. So I decided to put the phone in the bedroom. Still, there was a handful of people I'd give my number to. I didn't want to be awakened too early in the morning. Or too late at night.

The man installing the telephone said to me that it wouldn't be any problem for him to put a jack in each room. "That way," he said, "you can plug your phone into whichever place you want, when you want it." Actually it was a simple solution. And it cost only pennies a day.

I picked up the phone. Why all this impatience, why such feverishness? I dialed the number of the philosophy student. I suspected he wasn't a student any more. He had doubtless earned his degree the previous semester. The sky was clouding over. It was going to rain. A gray sky is most unpleasant: it fills me with anxiety. And when it remains overcast for any length of time, I have found there is only one solution: go out and tie one on. But for the moment I was still all right, sustained by my impatience and the hope that I would be speaking with the philosophy student. It was ringing. I waited. It didn't answer; I was more and more disappointed. I was still holding the receiver next to my ear. I had been right not to give up so easily. It was a woman's voice that answered.

"Isn't André there?" I asked, my voice ridden with anxiety.

"Yes, he's here. He just walked in."

I told him my name and asked if I was calling at a bad time. Was he sure I wasn't disturbing him? He told me that I wasn't, no, honestly, really, I swear you're not. He was pleased to hear from me. He even wanted to know how I was, how things had been going for me. Yes, he had passed his exams. He was teaching in a high school, and

at the same time working on his thesis. He had even considered asking my office, my ex-office, for my address. I
told him the office didn't know it. I said that for the past
two or three months I had been meaning to go by the office,
ex-office, to see my former colleagues and give them my
address, and also to invite them, some of them, to pay me
a visit. But each day I had postponed the trip, that veritable
adventure, putting off till tomorrow what I couldn't do
today. But now I had made up my mind once and for all.
I was overjoyed at the thought of going back there. I
chatted with him for a long time; he assured me he was in
no hurry, and asked me to tell him the story of my life.

I had the courtesy to ask him to tell me first about himself. Which he did. He was engaged to the girl who had
answered the phone. She was young, two years younger
than he, pretty and intelligent. She was still a student.

I told him that on my end things were fine, really fine.
I was enjoying my life of leisure. It was true there were
moments when I was bored. I hadn't been going to the
movies. That was a failing. I wanted to go. Reading?
Hardly at all. But I had every intention of reading from
now on, because other people and what they said, and
problems in general, were beginning to interest me. Besides, everything is interesting to some degree, that's a
foregone conclusion. There are no "degrees" of interest that
we can have for people or things. It wasn't a question of
hierarchy: if you preferred one thing to another, or one person to another, that was a matter of subjective judgment.

He said to me (was he making fun of me?) that being
alone had made me more profound, adding that he could
tell I had done a great deal of thinking. After that I talked

to him about mundane things. I talked to him about my concierge, who at first had looked at me strangely, as if I were some strange creature. She had clearly taken a strong dislike to me. No, I did not have a persecution complex. I had given her some little presents, I had tipped her a few times, too. She had taken the money, but it was as though in accepting it she had been humiliated. Every time I walked by she tried to give me a hard time. When I went out while she was sweeping the lobby I would track the dust from the stairs onto her clean floor. And when I came back while she was sweeping I would track the dust from the lobby onto the stairway. She scowled at me. Asked me questions that were vaguely indiscreet: "So it's you again! Where are you going this time? You always seem to be going out. And yet it's safe to say you're not going to work. You're lucky. Not like the rest of us." And then that hostility, that mistrust slowly disappeared. It might still be there, but at least you couldn't see it any more. She had grown used to my comings and goings at the same time every day, and adjusted to my strange solitude. "You look to me," she said to me at one point, "like you're hiding from the police. Or from some rivals." I told her that no one was after my skin, that as far as my hash was concerned I was sure no one was trying to settle it, and that I had never belonged to the underworld. "Just as I suspected," she said, "you don't look brave enough for that." But now it was over. I didn't irritate her any longer, perhaps for the simple reason that I didn't interest her any more. That much I sensed. Now she responded, when I doffed my hat in passing, for I was in the habit of wearing a hat, by an automatic nod of her head. I wondered if she really saw me. In any case, she no longer looked at me. I was part of the building, like the floors and the landings. Not the way it used to be, when she would lift one corner of the curtain on her glass door to scowl out at me. Scowl is hardly a strong enough term. I had a cleaning woman, Jeanne, who was forever telling me the story of her life. Stories, rather. I'm fed up with that one, let me tell you. She hadn't changed from the day she began: talk talk talk. She chewed my ear off, *hurt* my ears, kept me from daydreaming, from thinking, it was just as bad as the first day, worse in fact; it hadn't changed. It was hard to sneak away; she called me back, took me by my suitcoat button. In vain I had tried to tiptoe out, but she had an acute sense of hearing. "But does all that interest you?" I asked the person on the other end of the line. "I'm going on like Jeanne." "No, no," he answered, "it interests me, your case interests me." He was a philosopher, but he was also a psychologist, a psychoanalyst. Being a psychologist, spending your life worrying about others, is extraordinary, truly extraordinary: the vocation of listening to others!

"In other words, things are going well for you, more or less?"

"Yes," I answered. "I venture to say they are. Sometimes I still have the feeling that I'm separated from the rest of the world, the impression that I'm in a kind of glass cage. That, of course, is a bore. Actually, it was boredom I had to struggle against, among other things, when I didn't feel as though I were in a glass cage, when morally I stretched out a helping hand to other people the glass walls retreated, and it seemed to me as though it were the whole universe that was surrounded with invisible walls. Through which, however, you couldn't see. . . . The sky was a vault, and beyond the houses, beyond the city and the countryside that stretched behind, lay the horizon, the closed door of the horizon. Does all that seem normal? Time was short and long at the same time, at least that was the way it seemed to me: the seconds were interminable, each second an excoriation, and the years were short. It all passed. I know, there's nothing new about that: everyone regrets the passage of time, more or less. But for me that contradiction was impossible. I was so overwhelmed with the weight of the moment that I had never had any chance to take advantage of it, not to mention enjoy it. Other people also have sad faces, which portray boredom and despair. Do you think that all I'm doing is projecting my own feelings, and clothing other people in my own terrible depression? Do you think that other people are happy, that they are carefree, or that they have concerns, some big, some small, that nonetheless don't overpower them? Do you think that other people are living? That's not normal, is it? I'd be better off working, but doing what? I certainly can't go back to the office and put in my eight hours a day. I prefer being slightly worried. Besides, it's not as if I were worried all the time, I don't spend the whole day fretting. There is, to be sure, the moment of waking. That, I admit, is painful. Another day ahead of me, a vast, deserted beach as far as the eye can see. Farther. But I do get up, I do make and drink my coffee. It's Jeanne who will wash the cup and saucer, and the pan. And when I drink my coffee, I'd have to say in all fairness that it is a pleasant moment. See, I do have pleasant moments. The pleasant ones are fleeting. What I have to do is find a way to make them deeper and last longer. There are spurts of joy and happiness. But no sooner do they come than they are gone. But if there are these spurts, it means there is some inexhaustible well, there is a fountain somewhere, perhaps a lake too, a sparkling new lake surrounded by white mountains whose slopes lie golden in the sun, gilded too by the light of some internal paradise. That ought to exist, somewhere. I tell myself it should, I tend to believe it, at least to some degree, I believe it less, I don't believe it at all. The deeper I go, the more I find only sludge. Silt and slime. A foul pond. I'm contradicting myself. That means favorable thrusts are still occurring inside, something akin to a struggle. I'm not always overwhelmed; not always engulfed. I know that the world is always and indefatigably virgin. That's what gives me what passes for a reason for living. But even what I know I don't know well enough, not with all my heart and soul. Whereas the weight or the breadth come without my having to think about it, as though it were the essence and matter of everything."

In answer, he told me that of course he still had plenty of time to chat with me, no courses to teach today, I could go on for a few more seconds. Even longer. My case, he declared, was well known to psychotherapists. He cited me several examples, which weren't all that rare, where the patients had the impression that the entire universe was excremental.

I replied that fortunately I hadn't reached that stage yet. Only mud, slime, and silt, but also a pure lake, and snows on gentle slopes. Normal people are somewhere between the two. Neither light nor shadows. They go busily about their affairs, their concerns, their daily preoccupations in an area between darkness and light; they live off that. People live off that. That's what being human implies. Not me: I can live only in a state of grace. Who ever lives in a state of grace? And yet not to live in a state of grace is inadmissible. For me, there is no middle ground between grace and shit. Other people are calm and collected, more or less. They grow accustomed to that absence. I ask too much of it, I'm too full of the sin of pride; I think only of myself. Why don't I think about other people? There's the rub, there's the real sticking point. Other people accept the situation they've been saddled with. They only suffer when some catastrophe strikes; the death of one of their loved ones, war, famine, sickness. I have to confess that those things also interest me. Perhaps I ought to be ashamed to admit it, but it draws me out of my torpor. With a mixture of impatience and pleasure I await the arrival of the maid, knowing she will be bringing the morning paper. I fall on the paper and literally revel in it, devour it, delight in it, in a morose way admittedly, but delectation nonetheless, as I read the headlines that talk of war, atrocities, fires, floods, and pollution on the rise through the world and very likely to asphyxiate us all. A mixture of fear and fascination. That helps me get through a good half hour every morning. It's lively, or thrilling. Having imbibed all the news of the day, there's still the crosswood puzzle. That takes another good hour. Which brings us almost to apéritif time, after which it's lunchtime, followed by a little nap. Two or three difficult hours to get through till dinnertime, and after dinner, home, where I sink into a deep sleep. The next morning, the same distress, and then comes coffee, I regain my faculties, such as they are, and the whole cycle begins again. You can see that I've mapped out my days with a certain amount of care. But then this, more than anything else there is this: the amazement that I exist and that things exist. But more than anything else there is that inability to conceive of the infinite. It doesn't help you to live, but I can't stop asking myself the question. And of course, you say all that's banal, commonplace. And probably it is. Born in horror and pain, I also live in horrible dread of the end, the exit. I'm caught in an incredible, inadmissible, infernal trap, between two frightful events.

He answered by saying that everything I was describing was, in fact, quite ordinary, quite familiar. I ought to read more, or simply read, since I didn't read at all. I might want to consult the agnostics, whose teachings might prove instructive. And, you know, everyone had posed these same questions at one time or another. There's nothing new about them at all.

"Of course," I answered, "I'm sure you're aware of these problems; you've read a lot, you have a great fount of knowledge. But for me these questions are crucial, they take me and shake me. For you, they're only cultural. You don't wake up every morning with fear and trembling, asking yourself what the answers are, then telling yourself there aren't any. But you know that everyone has asked himself these same questions. And you also know that no one has ever come up with any answers, because there aren't any. The only difference is that for you the whole thing is files and catalogues. Since you know that these questions have been raised, and you know who raised them and what books and treatises have dealt with them, you don't worry your head about them any longer, you've put them aside, filed them away somewhere in your memory. Yes, you have; for you, it's part of your culture. Despair

has been domesticated; people have turned it into litera-
ture, into works of art. That doesn't help me. It's part of
culture, part of culture. So much the better for you if culture has succeeded in exorcising man's drama, his tragedy."
He told me that we'd have to talk more about the whole
subject, that I ought to come and see him. But now he
couldn't talk any longer, he had to go out, he was after all
a professional man. I was an obsessional neurotic. It wasn't
normal to go on harping endlessly on the same subject. He
knew someone who might be able to help me. Metaphysical
anxiety was his diagnosis: when metaphysical anxiety
reaches the proportions it has in my case, he said, treat-
ment is clearly called for. There are all kinds of pills that
will cure metaphysical anxiety. Chemotherapy as practiced
today had also been known to produce remarkable results.
He hung up. I thought that it was strange for him to
assume that it was abnormal for anyone to be forever asking questions about the nature of the universe, about what
the human condition really was, *my* condition, what I was
doing here, if there was really something to do. It seemed
to me on the contrary that it was abnormal for people *not*
to think about it, for them to allow themselves to live, as it
were, unconsciously. Perhaps it's because everyone, all the
others, are convinced in some unformulated, irrational way
that one day everything will be made clear. Perhaps there
will be a morning of grace for humanity. Perhaps there will
be a morning of grace for me.

Before I fell asleep, before I plunged into the yawning
abyss, there were times when in my semi-lucid state I
smiled at the thought that perhaps, a few hours from then,

dawn would bring me knowledge and release, and that dawn would be eternal. Sometimes at night I thought about it. Only sometimes, though, for most of the time I would come home drunk, oblivious, insensate, but liberated from my obsession for the insoluble and incurable. And the mornings, the long succession of mornings, never brought the one I had dreamed about, the one I kept hoping for. With it came a feeling of great bitterness, which the doctor would doubtless ascribe to my liver. All the same, it was a bitterness I couldn't get rid of. I tried to go back to sleep, to make my sleep last as long as I could, so that night and sleep would never end. The perspective of the long day ahead of me, which was already taking hold of me, the thought that for hours on end I would have to battle, not always successfully, against boredom and worry, was more than I could cope with. Everything was painful, the slightest gesture, the sight of these walls with their flower print, and the bedspread to match. But I had to be up and about before Jeanne arrived. She worked, she was up at the crack of dawn, I was ashamed of my idleness, or that moral paralysis. I put one foot out of bed, then the second, and struggled up. It was as if I were carrying my own body, which was a dead weight; I was a prisoner of my own distress. The idea of washing up struck me as a job just as tough as that of a common laborer. I went into the bathroom as if I were a prisoner on death row. That lasted for half an hour. In the old days, I used to wash with cold water. Now it was impossible, more than I could bear. I always stepped into my bath with a feeling akin to dread, a fear that doubtless symbolized for me a fear of water that went back very far. I had the feeling that the bathtub, filled with water, was a sort of grave. Going into the water was like burying myself alive. And after that I still had to shave. I stood there gazing at myself in the mirror for a long time before I went about the task at hand. I ran my hand over my face. I felt the stubble on my cheeks and chin; in places it was already turning white. I looked at myself, and I didn't like what I saw: that oversized nose; these pale blue, lusterless eyes; the face slightly puffy; the uncombed hair, which was too long, because I didn't go to the barber very often; the oversized ears; the wrinkles in the puffy surface. No one, but no one was like me; everyone ought to see that I wasn't like other people. That peculiarity must have been embarrassing. And yet there was nothing abnormal about my face. I was like the others without being like the others. I had to assume that the unusual quality of my character showed through my skin. And yet people didn't look at me in the street; people didn't turn around to look at me as they passed by. That's not quite true. A few did: the concierge; my neighbor with her little dog; Jeanne, the cleaning lady, who shook her head every time she looked at me; and then there was the waitress in the restaurant, whose behavior with respect to me was quite special: a dash of friendship mixed with a pinch of disdain. Other people normally didn't look me in the eye. And if they did, hostility was what I read in their expressions, hostility toward me. Yes, that was it: they are all hostile toward me, hostile or indifferent. But I also feel the same hostility and the same indifference toward them. What did they have against me? The fact that I didn't live the way they did; that I refused to resign myself to my fate. And what did I have against them? Nothing. Especially when I came to the conclusion that when all was said and done they were like me. They were me. That's why I disliked them: because they were the others without being completely the others. If they had really been different from me, I could have modeled myself after them. I would have found that helpful. I had the feeling that I was bearing within me all the fear and anxiety of billions of human beings, the malaise of the entire human race. If the conditions had been different, each of them would have experienced the same anxiety, the same fear of life, the same malaise. But they chose not to; they preferred not to go too deeply into the subject. They live out their lives, from adolescence through adulthood and on into old age, in a state of unawareness or resignation, of unconscious resignation. They stand up to themselves as best they can, as long as they can. But if everyone plumbed the depths, each would experience the fear and anxiety of billions of human beings. The anxiety resides in each one of us. That strikes me as one of the fundamental acts of cruelty on the part of the divinity: each person is simultaneously unique and everyone; each person is universal. It would have been so much easier to distribute all the anxiety, despair, and panic equally among the billions of creatures on the face of the earth. In that case, our portion of anxiety would only be one three billionth of the total amount of universal suffering. But no, in dying each of us bears with him the entire crumbling universe.

I prepared my shaving instruments—I didn't use an electric shaver—then soaped my face. I tried to smoke while I was shaving, a neat trick if you can do it, and when I had finished—shaving, that is—I felt greatly relieved. It was as though I had overcome some great obstacle. If Jeanne had not yet arrived, I would make a mad dash to the living room, open the sideboard and toss down my two glasses of brandy, which for me was like inflating a balloon. But if Jeanne was there, she would see me do it and lecture me about it, to my great embarrassment. Getting up early in the morning has its virtues.

I no longer knew where I was. At the same time I did know, of course. I had the feeling that I was there and at the same time wasn't there. It seemed to me that it was changing, or had changed. A bizarre change, easy to feel or immediately felt, but impossible to put into words. It was my house, the same house, the same chair, the same sofa, the same rug, and yet it was not the same rug or the same sofa or the same books or the same walls. Inexplicably strange. Or rather a strangeness which meant that basically I had failed to express it clearly. And yet the world was not the same. The location of objects was different. The sky had changed, so had people. And yet it was something else. Who was I? Where was I? An inexpressible anxiety, since words themselves were no longer capable of saying the same thing. I could move about as before, walk to the kitchen, descend the stairs, go out and buy something I needed, come back, but all that was taking place in a world that was no longer the same world.

When this change was taking place, some time ago, I was filled with a kind of joy. Now I felt only fear. I suddenly found myself uprooted and transplanted somewhere else in a customary world. As if the world could be customary! As if the world could be normal! As if breathing and feeling your own heart beat were natural! I looked at an object in front of me, roughly six feet tall and four feet wide, with a double door that opened. Inside there were hangers on which clothes, my clothes, were hanging, and shelves on which linen was folded. Obviously, if anyone asked me what this object was, I would have answered that it was a closet. But it wasn't a closet any more, and yet it wasn't something else, either. No matter how many people asked, I would always have replied: a closet. And yet the words were lying. Not only were the objects no longer the same objects, but words weren't the same words, either. Words struck me as false. Objects, or so it seemed to me, had lost their purpose. I still made use of them, but I had the feeling they weren't meant to be used for that purpose, and even that they no longer had any function at all. It was as though I did not have the right to touch them. I was plunged headlong into a new world that I didn't know what to do with. A world that wasn't meant to be useful. Whatever world it was, whether a parallel world or the world contrary to ours, a negative to our positive, it wasn't mine, it couldn't be mine. Where had they taken me? The world swayed. One entity had been substituted for another. I was in another creation. It seemed as though I was in another creation. I had to learn what things meant and how they worked all over again. But to learn how something works does not reveal its essence. And all things around me were the others. And I was another. Wasn't the floor going to cave in? I rejected everything. Wasn't I too going to be rejected in turn? Rejected from what? Into what? And what could that "what" and that "into what" be? If I tried to open a book and read it, things that had once struck me as being ordinary and commonplace now leapt out at me, strange and inexplicable. I would touch a pedestal table, and wonder why in the world it was called that, and what it meant. Where had I come from? Who was who? When that state of mind didn't fill me with fear, it made me uncomfortable. A feeling of not being in your own place. A feeling of not having a place to yourself. A feeling of not having any self. Move your hands and look at them. Doing that doubtless brought me back to a state of infancy, the child who looks at his hands without knowing what they are. If that experiment had been conducted in a happy frame of mind, as though it were a discovery, I would have been happy myself. There were times in the past when discoveries would fill me with pleasure. But now they no longer did. Now joy was foreign to me, no longer affected me. Joy was suddenly realizing, in a way I might describe as supernatural, that the world is there, that you are there in the world, that one exists, that I exist. Now everything seemed to prove the inexistence of things and my own inexistence. I was afraid of disappearing. By looking and listening carefully at the window or in the living room, I had the impression that the little seismic disturbances, imperceptible but fairly numerous, had made the world extremely fragile. Everything was disintegrating, everything seemed on the verge of sinking into an ordinary void. The universe where reality was less and less resistant. Would there be something behind that scenery? Would there be something, another setting? Or nothing at all? And what was that "nothing at all"? I felt myself teetering in a world about to topple. Strange how everything is simultaneously so present and so absent, so hard, so thick, and so fragile. Did it really exist? Had it ever existed? One more straw, slightly heavier than the rest, would break not only the camel's back, but everything, into thousands of pieces. I felt as though I were one of the points of light in a huge display of fireworks. The nausea of nothingness. And then the nausea of surfeit. How could such a situation continue, and if it could for how much longer, assuming time was still there. Perhaps it wasn't; perhaps there were only instantaneous moments.

I sat down in my chair. Mechanically I picked up my newspaper. Crimes, wars, felonies and misdemeanors, film advertisements: nothing. How could this nothing weigh so heavily? And how could that heaviness at the same time be so light? Too material and yet immaterial, too. This world, made out of papier-mâché, this particular theatrical setting could be substituted for any other at any time. I pictured this world in which I was one of the actors. Author perhaps, or simply one of the players. Carefully, I got to my feet, put on my hat, slipped into my coat, and went downstairs, trembling at every step. I walked down the street, staggered would be more accurate, from time to time touching the walls, simultaneously fearing that they might crush me or that they might vanish. I reached the restaurant. The waitress looked at me and said that I must be sick, that my eyes had a wild look about them. It seemed to me that it was she who looked distraught. I let myself slump into my usual chair, at my usual table. I gazed out the window and for some time watched the fleeting silhouettes which seemed to emerge from the thick fog only to plunge back into it again and disappear.

"You don't look very well, Monsieur. Again today, Monsieur, if I may say so."

"Again today? Today even less than the other days. If there are any other days."

"Other days have existed. Other days will exist in the future. You give me the feeling you're in a fog."

"You're in a fog."

The waitress looked at me. "What's the matter with you? You ought to go see your doctor."

"Are you sure you exist?"

The waitress's eyes grew round. "I think so. Are you trying to frighten me? You exist too, I assure you."

"You know, there may be nothing beyond all that," I said, pointing to the windows, the walls, the street.

"What do you want to be beyond them? They're there, that's all."

"And you think that's all there is? It wouldn't be enough. It's a mere pittance. What do you think sustains all that?"

She looked at me in dismay. She liked me all right, but she always thought I was a little crazy.

"You're always ill at ease, as though you weren't in your own skin. You're going to answer that you can say that I don't know whether or not I have a skin. Or what skin is."

She hurried away from the table, to return moments later with my brandy. "Here," she said, "this will do you some good. It'll make you feel better."

I gulped down the glass of brandy. I did feel a little warmer. I said to her: "Do you think all this will go on much longer?"

"What do you mean, all this?"

"All this!"

"I can assure you it won't disappear from one day to the next. It will still be with us for a long time to come. Long after we're dead and gone, it will still be here."

"And when it topples, after it *is* gone, what will be in its place? Will there be something else? Don't you see that everything's disappearing on all sides? No, you don't see."

"I feel myself fairly well settled. And I work hard. The more you work, the more things there are. If there were fewer, perhaps it would be easier."

"And where will these things go?"

"You're asking me such crazy questions! Questions nobody can answer. I've never given such things any thought. And I don't intend to start now. People seem to scare you. But you scare me. . . . I'm scared for you. Your nerves are shot. But that's not too serious. Go and see your doctor. He can fix you up. Here's another glass of brandy."

"Don't you think that doctors are sick? We know that we're only here for a short stretch of time, that we're all going to die, and they tell you you're crazy if you think about death, if you're ridden with worry and anxiety. They're the ones who ought to be locked up. I'm the one whose thinking is normal, not them. They're abnormal."

"I'm going to cook you a good st.ak," she said. "With french fries."

"Make it well-done, if you don't mind."

I watched the other customers arriving. They sat down; they thought their manner was free and easy.

"Don't you see," I said, "they're all locked in glass coffins."

They looked at me. The waitress came over and whispered to me: "Keep still. They'll lock you up."

The fact was, there was a certain uproar in the restaurant, and eyes turning to look at me.

"Lock me up? I already am locked up. Like everyone else. Locked up and at the same time too free. The crystal is invisible."

I left the restaurant, feeling their looks follow me out the door. I started off in the direction of the big square, which I still hadn't explored. It was a good distance away, well over a mile. Had it been there for a long time, or had they invented it recently? The square was swarming with people. Another battle. There were two opposing crowds battling each other, with the police caught in between. Caught and crushed. Insults succeeded blows. Blows succeeded insults. Crushing blows, club and bludgeon blows on the head. There were crackling sounds, explosions, brains spilled from brain pans, and from the invisible glass boxes. People were stabbing one another. I can't figure out how they always managed to be three against one. The square was strewn with the dead and wounded. From all four streets that emptied into it, vans packed with police poured into the square. They too were encased in invisible glass coffins, which also surrounded their helmets. I threw myself into the thick of the crowd and shouted:

"You're already in your coffins. Don't be in such a rush to go about hitting people. Are you really in so much of a hurry? If you are, why are you? At the rate you're going there soon won't be anyone left."

No one heard me, or no one wanted to hear me. The pavements and sidewalks of the square were turning into a strange porridge. Heads were exploding into a thousand pieces, as were the cars and trucks. I shouted:

"We can also go down without all this sound and fury. We can go down peacefully. The disintegration doesn't have to be so brutal. Well, to every man his own choice."

I melted into the crowd. All around me arms were flailing, club were striking, but not a single blow landed on me. It was as though they didn't see me. For them I was only a ghost. They were ghosts, too: troubled, violent ghosts. I tried to hold one person's arm to keep it from striking, to restrain another's foot from kicking. The police had joined in and were taking part in the battle with their nightsticks, their capes, and their shields. It was impossible to tell which side they were on. Unless they were against both sides.

I managed to climb the steps of the pedestal on which the statue in the middle of the square was perched. From that vantage point I shouted:

"Listen to me! Listen! I'm your arbitrator. We can work things out. You can work things out among yourselves. But not like this! Let's sit down and reason together. This can all be worked out on a friendly basis."

I didn't win a single brawler over to my viewpoint. On all sides, they continued to drop like flies. Again I shouted to them:

"We can work this whole thing out in a friendly way. Pick some delegates. Then tell your delegates what it is you want. I see, I understand; you don't really want to come to any understanding. Why are you in such a hurry? Why are you in such an awful hurry?"

I was speaking to the void. A mixture of void and fullness. I was speaking to the void. Or to the overly full. I gave it another try:

"I'm a man too, just like you. I speak the same language you do."

But I didn't speak the same language. I had managed to grasp the statue around the waist, and from this new perch I went on shouting. They certainly had no excuse for not seeing me. As little excuse as they had for not hearing me. I have a good set of lungs, and my arms and legs are on the long side. They took me for a scarecrow. More likely, they took me for nothing at all. There could be no doubt about it: they must not have seen me. Except for one policeman, who asked me:

"What are you doing there?"

Then he went back to his head-splitting chores.

Slowly I climbed back down among them, and tried to collar a few:

"You're crazy," I said. "If you're not, tell me what it is you want. I'll work it out."

They wasted no time slipping out of my grip. One of them, a man alone, said to me:

"You're the one who's crazy. You don't understand that we're fighting for our rights."

"For our freedom," another one chimed in.

I asked them what rights they were referring to. I asked them what sort of freedom they were demanding. Neither one answered me. They too turned and went back to their head-splitting activities.

The whole area was filled with blood and glass. Things were turning more and more violent every minute. People were still streaming into the square from all four streets. Some people were climbing down from the balconies of their houses. There were some who slid down the rainpipes from their garrets. Alone in the surging crowd, I wrung my hands:

"But I tell you, it's all very simple. It could all be very simple."

Someone else shouted back: "If it were all that simple, it wouldn't be so complicated."

Those who fell with their heads split open had a blissful look about them. Those who were doing the skull-splitting had a happy, victorious air about them. There were times when the latter, the happy head-splitters, had their own heads cracked open later on.

Finally, a heavyset man came over to me and said:

"You don't seem to understand that this is a civil war."

He went back to his stabbing.

So that's what a civil war looked like. He heard me shout after him:

"That means you want to kill."

"That means we're fed up. That we can't take it any more."

"All you need to do is change the institutions," I shouted. "But that wouldn't be enough for you!" Then I added: "I said, changing the institutions isn't enough for you. All institutions, all societies, are bad. Just read the newspapers. I ask you, is there a good one among them? Are there *any* good societies? War is a holiday, a treat, and it's a holiday you want. . . . Did you know," I went on shouting, "'that the only happy songs in Mexico are the revolutionary songs? Revolutions for this side, revolutions for that side, all kinds of revolutions. Revolutions for, revolutions against, it makes no difference. Just so long as people kill and are killed. I know that life doesn't exist. I know that nothing really exists. All I see is a mass of people clubbing and being clubbed. Non-existence is bloody. We're not alive. That's odd. People kill and are killed in order to prove to themselves that life exists. But there's nothing, I say, there's nothing, nothing," I shouted with all the strength I could muster. I looked around and saw that there was nobody there. A big empty square. A big square in a big city, and yet it looked like a square in some provincial town. Had I actually seen those men and women wielding clubs, bludgeoning one another to death? Had I seen the police vans? Had I seen the blood on the ground? Had I heard the militant songs, the happy holiday songs? Where were the monsters? And where was their mirth, their gaiety?

An old man came over to me and said:

"What you thought you just saw here really took place over two hundred years ago. This square is called Revolution Square. Of a future revolution, one yet to come, one likely to come. Go on home. Everything comes out the same in the end. Today, there are other institutions against which we plan to fight. It's not for today. Tomorrow, perhaps. Perhaps it was yesterday. One of my ancestors fought and had his head split open; another fought right here, on this very square. The first ancestor didn't die of his wounds; he only died much later. At home. The story goes it was his wife who poisoned him. Not for any political reasons, though, not over any institutions."

Taking me by the elbow, the old man guided me to the far side of the square, from where I was able to retrace my steps back down the street which led to my restaurant.

Dazed and bewildered by the noises I had heard, frightened by the pieces of broken glass and the fallen bodies, shell-shocked from the blows that people had dealt not to me but to others, I opened the restaurant door. The only person still there was the waitress.

"Where are the customers imbedded in their glass coffins? Were they all killed during the Revolution?"

She looked at me apprehensively.

"They ate and left. They may have got into arguments somewhere; perhaps they started killing one another; perhaps they're all going to come back here tonight for their apéritif, to have dinner, to chat. I didn't hear any noise."

"That's not all there is, believe me. There's more than noise. Look, my hands are covered with blood, and yet I didn't murder anyone."

"That's only paint. You must have touched some walls that were freshly painted. Give me your hands. I'll wipe them off with a damp cloth." She looked at me, and her eyes were filled with infinite pity. She said: "You're upset. Your nerves are all shot."

"You're the one who ought to be upset. You're crazy if you aren't. You don't know what's going on around you. Even I have only the vaguest notion of what's going on, the very faintest notion."

"You keep to yourself too much, Monsieur."

"I'm surrounded by people. I'm surrounded by the crowd. By the crowd or by nothing."

While she was wiping my hands, she repeated:

"You keep to yourself too much, Monsieur, you really do. You need a woman. If you want me. . . ."

She kissed me. I was the one who should've taken the

initiative, I was thinking. But it was nice anyway. And it seemed to me so true, so real.

She moved in with me. The bed was big enough. She had plenty of room. In the morning, it was very pleasant to see bare breasts in the sunlight. Once in a while she frightened me. There were times at night when I couldn't fall asleep, and once when she fell asleep, snoring ever so lightly, her nightgown inched up above her spread thighs. The female organ has always struck me as being a kind of nether wound tucked between the thighs. Something like a pit, a yawning abyss, but above all like an open wound: vast, incurable, and deep. The impression it made on me was always one of fear and pity. An abyss, yes, that was the term. Gently, I covered it. She didn't even wake up. Like a sleepwalker, I went on wandering aimlessly through the apartment. I smoked cigarette after cigarette, I who had almost forgotten how to smoke, until I was so tired I couldn't keep my eyes open any longer and I climbed back into bed beside her, keeping as far away from her wound as possible, trying to forget her wound, lying on the edge of that portion of the bed reserved for me. I ended by falling asleep, on my right side.

Despite the long, hard hours she put in at the restaurant downstairs, she also took care of the house, and I had fired the maid. The neighbors felt less self-conscious about me now that they saw a woman living with me. They smiled pleasantly when they passed, looking more relaxed and happy. I seemed more normal to them, less worrisome. I was fond of that woman, with her broad smile that bespoke a hearty constitution, although a trace of fatigue could be detected in some of her features. Every morning she sang in her bath. I never sang. I didn't even whistle. I was 'the victim of a frightful pain that apparently wasn't justified. And to think that, to my way of thinking, health and normality remained to be proved.

When I awoke in the morning, before she did, I felt a kind of deep-rooted happiness, something I hadn't felt for a long time. A very distant memory welled up within me, clear and yet vague, shadow and color simultaneously. It was something very far removed in time and yet infinitely close, very strange and yet completely familiar, true and false, it was . . . a long time ago, a long time ago. And then some event . . . I couldn't remember any longer what it was, something had happened. And in front of that half-clear, half-dark image a kind of whirlwind. There were times when I wondered whether she and I weren't the basis for a new world. A world restored. A world without flaw or fissure. A safe world, one where God had done a successful job. Scholar friends of mine once told me that it is written in the cabala that God had already tried twenty-seven times to create the universe. This apparently was the twentieth-eighth and least unsuccessful effort. It made you wonder what the earlier twenty-seven must have been like. When will He ever manage to make a good one? I have the impression He's already given up on this one, number twenty-eight, and that He's allowing us to sink into the abyss of the void. Another theory has it that we're only a tenuous island which may not even be connected to the definitive universe. The things you hear about the world! Mornings, at dawn, while she was still asleep, funeral processions, fabulously funereal, loaded down with flowers, wreaths, and all sorts of inscriptions, passed back and forth in front of my windows. There were tall men in black with top hats, and tall women in full mourning regalia, with black veils over their faces. Once I woke her up:

"Come and see," I shouted to her, "come and see what's going by right under our noses."

She got up, still half-asleep, then went back to bed, saying that I was seeing things, that I was dreaming with my eyes open. At other times, for weeks on end nothing went by, despite my vigil.

After hastily washing, she dressed, and went off to work. I couldn't refrain from noticing how chapped and cracked her hands were. She never had any time; I on the other hand had all the time in the world. I drank the café au lait that she had prepared for me before she had left, laced with a little brandy or rum, then dressed in my own good time. I didn't see her again till lunch time, at the restaurant. In her waitress role, scurrying to and fro in response to the customers' demands, it was as if she were another person. Then came the meal itself. Followed by the futile attempt to go out and, as she put it, take a little turn, go and see some friends. I tried but I couldn't; I went back to the house to wait for evening apéritif time, then dinner, then the walk back home with her. There were times when she gave me all kinds of advice, but that was happening less and less often. Most of the time we didn't exchange a word as we walked. We walked down our street arm in arm, climbed the stairs, and went inside. I made a vague effort to read the newspaper, but my consuming desire made it impossible to concentrate. I waited until she had finished undressing, then lay down feverishly beside her. Love was like a pier extending out into the abyss, a kind of despair, a way of dying stoically. Then we fell asleep immediately. But I would awake a short time later and begin pacing back and forth again throughout the apartment, a cigarette in my hand. And suddenly I was seized with a fearful thought: how long was she going to put up with this life? How long? I would ask myself time and time again. She's a healthy woman. She can't put up for very long with someone the doctors would classify as depressive.

Once in a while I thought about asking her to quit her job. Then I decided not to. She wasn't looking for anything from me, but I did have enough money to take care of her. I wasn't sure, though, that she and I were really Adam and Eve incarnate. Reincarnate. And what if we were! Think of the work that would entail. That thought led to another, namely that if I were a new Adam it would be as though I were a new Atlas. And that would go on for centuries and centuries. The very idea of fathering Cain filled me with panic. What a stupid idea, I said in my darker moments, wanting to start in all over again just when we're almost at the end, when it's so easy to have done with it. There was also the regret about what might have been, what we didn't experience. So many acts, so many adventures, so many loves, so many things that escaped us because we aren't careful enough and because we don't know how to live and follow the fullness of days to enter and overwhelm us. In short, all that was pure fiction. Memories that went back to the edifying books I had read as a child.

To have the waitress with me was for the time being enormously useful. Her chapped and cracked hands were painful to behold, but if only she would take a little care of them they could become beautiful again. She was rather petite, and very pretty. Lovely black eyes with long lashes, a face whose features were a trifle coarse. If only I could have her with me all the time, for the rest of my life, to the very end, she doubled over and I hardly able to walk at all, even with a cane. I found the vision horrifying. All I had to do was look out the window: hundreds of old men were walking by in the street below, all with their canes and their bent backs. I wondered if they were going to meet somewhere farther along? I remembered a meeting of old people. Between their hacking coughs, they were extolling the beauties of life and proclaiming their rights, to other old men of higher rank than they, further demanding that the restrictive laws regarding age be changed so that they could go back to their jobs. I was older than any of them.

The idea that I might be able to provide the waitress with a better life was interwoven with all the above. What should I do? Since for the moment things were going well, that is not as badly as they might have gone. We'd see how things went tomorrow. Perhaps she and I would both die very suddenly. She, rather. The idea that I might have an accident frightened me to death, and it took me forever before I could bring myself to cross the street.

When she woke up, I said to her with a broad smile, and the feeling that I was being extremely generous: "I've been meaning to tell you for some time now: I have enough money, if you'd prefer not going to work any more. I have enough money, you know."

In answer, she said she had been expecting me to make some such a proposal for a while now, actually since we had started living together. The problem was, as I had hesitated earlier, so now she wasn't sure any longer. She had the impression she was living with a depressive. It wasn't easy, taking care of me, always trying to cheer me up. No, it wasn't easy. She preferred working and not having any obligations, and besides she wasn't sure whether she was going to stay with me much longer. Someone had offered her another job. What was more, she found this "someone" rather attractive.

"You want to leave me? Soon?"

I was engulfed by a huge wave of regret, of bitterness. I had happiness right here beside me. Once again, I hadn't known what to do with it. Fate wants to help me, providence sends her angels my way, and what do I do? Either I don't see them, or I reject them. The streets and gardens must be filled with fountains of life that I failed to see. Unquestionably, they must be there. When I went outside, I stretched out my arms to see if I could by any chance discover one of them. The weather was dry; not a drop of water anywhere. The people passing by screamed insults at me. And yet I went on walking, my arms still out, desperately hoping to find life, and fearing, with equal desperation, that I would soon be left alone. To live with a depressive is harder work than hard work. I could still hear those words that she had uttered one day. When I reached the restaurant, there she was, setting and clearing the tables as if everything were just fine. It seemed to me that I was living a double life: on one hand something was going on, in that kind of eternity of the commonplace; on the other hand, a major disruption had occurred, a huge hole had been dug. After dinner I waited for her as usual; we walked home together, as usual. She didn't say a word to me. But her face had changed, it was the face of a statue, someone who has a secret. It was from one of the other customers at the restaurant that I learned she was going to leave the place. That night we didn't say a word to each other. I kept waiting and watching for a word, a look. It was only the next morning, at breakfast, that she told me she was leaving. I had spent a terrible night, tossing and turning half the time, unable to fall asleep, and then when I did I had troubled dreams and nightmares. I was, I won't say ready for the news when it came, but in the spirit. I had dreamed that the world was receding beneath my feet at a dizzying rate, and that I was all out of breath running to try to overtake it. I was on a narrow footbridge above the abyss. I wanted to take off, jump and fall heavily among the thorns and brambles below, among the beasts below.

"I can't tell you how sorry I am to see you go," I finally managed.

"I'm terribly sorry that you're sorry," she said. "You never talked. You were so wrapped up in your own thoughts. I don't even know if they were thoughts. I mean thoughts like ours. You're not crazy, and yet you give the impression you are."

"It's because I'm right. . . . It's because I see and know. How can I explain it to you? Are you ever amazed to find yourself in the restaurant, or out in the street, or sitting across from me? Don't you find anything strange in all that? In all that," I said, raising my arms in a vague gesture meant to indicate the world around.

"You see," she said, "we're not made from the same cloth. We don't see things in the same way."

I was slumped deep into my chair, as though paralyzed. I watched her as she began to pack. One suitcase. Two suitcases. I heard her slam the closet door in the bedroom, then return and put some more belongings into her suitcase. I had the feeling her impending departure left her completely indifferent, that she took it with a grain of salt. I helped her close and lock her suitcases. Finally she said to me:

"It took me a long time to make up my mind. But you're too . . . too much the way you are. I thought that once you were with me your illness would get better."

"What illness?"

She put her fingers to her head. "You know, a little crazy. And yet I do like you, I still like you a lot. But I couldn't bear your silence, your air, those eyes of yours, like a scared monkey. And anyway, there's an end to everything."

I carried her suitcases downstairs. I hailed a taxi. And then I asked her:

"Who's going to wait on me at the restaurant?"

"My replacement. I've already talked to her about you. You'll see, she's very nice. I showed her which table was yours."

I had the feeling that I'd never be able to set foot in that restaurant again, that I would have to look for another place to eat; maybe I'd even have to move. But that would be more difficult. She kissed me good-bye, just brushing me with her lips, and with that she left.

It's strange. It was as though part of the world had suddenly collapsed and fallen into the abyss. What has become of the past, all those past lives, those ancient cathedrals, the crowds? Everything has fallen. It probably still exists somewhere, but if so we know nothing about it, victims of our own ignorance.

I found myself at the frontier of the world, the outer

limit. Ahead of me lay the bottomless hole of the uncreated. Behind me was the universe, pushing me with all its weight toward the abyss. It made one's head swim! I would have liked to back up. I was too afraid to move. One step forward would mean the fall; I would be seized, swallowed up, dissolved by the void. I closed my eyes, but that only made my dizziness and my nausea worse. The cosmos was teetering. Was this world too heavy, or too evanescent? It can disappear from one minute to the next. Or else crush me beneath its weight. Between the solid and the hollow, between plenitude and emptiness, I toppled over.

They helped me to my feet. The street was still there, with its same passersby, the same houses. I felt a young man's solid grip, his strong arm. He existed; I existed.

"Everything's right where it should be," I said. "It's amazing, Monsieur, everything is where it should be. Thank you for helping me."

"As it always has been, as it always will be. Don't worry; there's nothing to be afraid of."

"That's just it: it's that nothing I'm afraid of."

And yet the ground was solid. The young man's reassurances had had their effect on me. I was feeling better. My steps, at first hesitant, became steadier. For a few seconds, a kind of happiness. Perhaps nothing was lost, perhaps nothing would be lost. Perhaps time, as it marched on, would blend with eternity until they became one. Every few steps, I would touch the walls, wanting to feel their hard, dense reality. Perhaps what exists becomes identified with what is. Perhaps all this, this whole world, is insoluble reality, or the clothing of absolute reality. A simple curtain that conceals it. All these billions of pictures, all these billions of voices, whether synchronized or successive, are perhaps sustained by some immutable, basic foundations. That's a possibility. I desperately wanted it to be so. In all likelihood, I was missing some essential ingredient, some key. I wasn't like the others. Was there something wrong with me, something wrong with my mind? Other people walked peacefully behind me, beside me, in front of me: did they perhaps have some intuitive knowledge which had eluded me? I was the only one to be panic-stricken, in a state of perpetual panic, day after day after day, hour by hour, minute by minute, a nightmare; but I'll awake, I'll rediscover, behind what moves, the reality of what is unmoving.

People were walking past, brushing against me, looking at me as they passed. Were they shadows with eyes? Frightened looks, or reassuring. Passersby who were passing by, passing by.

I reached the restaurant. I sat down at my table. No, no, despite everything, everything is reassuring. The new waitress smiled as she brought me something to drink.

Suddenly the notion that the other waitress had left, that I would be alone once again, overwhelmed me. When the taxi had started to drive off, taking her with it, I had been as though stunned, in a state of near-shock. Only now was I clearly beginning to realize that she had left. And what about the period of time when she had been with me: had it really existed? Are those moments palpable? Are all those images obvious, all those memories true? All I was more or less sure of was what I could touch. Was what I had lived real or imaginary? It didn't exist any more. Perhaps it never existed. How could I make sure that memories weren't dreams, hallucinatory figments of my imagination? Smoke, all that, so much haze and mist; no, not even smoke: if only it could be smoke. Time will relegate these images to the void, to oblivion. It doesn't exist any more; it never did exist. It was nothing. There was nothing.

"She was a friend of yours, wasn't she?" I asked the new waitress.

"Of course. Don't worry, she'll let us know where she is and what she's doing."

I had polished off all my wine even before she brought the appetizer. I asked for some more. As usual, I gazed out the window at the passing parade in the street. All that will be gone, nothing will remain of it. How is it possible that what has existed no longer does? Where has it been then? Or where has what was gone to? Where has it been? Into what has it been swallowed? And yet you ought to be able to find it, it must be somewhere. Not even any dust. Yes, what was, if it was, cannot become extinct. And what did it mean to say that it wasn't any more? As I moved forward in time, I left it behind me. If I turned around to look back, from the heights of the present stage of flux, at the path already trod, all I would see would be mist. Perhaps if I turned back and retraced my steps I might be able to touch and experience again what was. Alas, it is as though what was had never been: the past, the pictures all out of focus, events all out of joint. Who can prove that it ever was? The past is a death without a body to prove it. Once upon a time . . . once upon a time.

I was going to be alone now. I felt the full impact of my misfortune. I drank a lot. I paid the bill, got to my feet, and said good-bye to the new waitress. I turned right, made it around the corner; I started down my own street; I reached the entrance of my house; I said hello to the concierge. She had seen that the other waitress had left. The concierge did not smile at me. She must figure that if the girl had left me, it had to be my fault. Because I was abnormal. Perhaps she would have liked to know more about it. I could have stopped and talked to her. I should have explained things to her. I decided to go up the stairs. For a long time I stood in front of my door, my key in my hand, hesitant. The lady downstairs came out with her dog. I made up my mind to open my door.

A slipper. I saw that she had forgotten one of her slippers. It was there, in the dark hallway. A trace. She had been there. She had lived here. The only tangible evidence of what was. How is it that the present becomes past? What is time anyway? The supplier of the void. Everything ought to be born present, immutable. I took the slipper in my hand. It was a witness. I took off my coat, my hat, and hung them on the rack in the dark hallway, then headed for the living room and slumped into the easy chair near the window. My apartment was a desert, as vast as the world. She had probably left because she had somebody else; she was going to meet somebody else. I felt something disagreeable, reminiscent of jealousy. Now that's odd. Was I really attached to her? Yes, of course I was. Which means that I had ties to the universe. The thought made me almost happy.

After a long period of calm, hostilities broke out again. For the time being, the battle was taking place on the square some distance from my street. Still, it was very likely that some people from my neighborhood were involved in the fighting. Not many, maybe two or three. One evening at dusk I saw one of them, his head all swathed in bandages. Another day, at one o'clock in the afternoon while I was having lunch in the restaurant, I saw another one, who arrived with his rifle slung across his back. Most of the customers hardly paid any attention to him, simply glancing up before going back to their eating. Some of them surrounded him at the bar, though. He ordered a *pastis*. The others followed suit. He had come there straight from the battle. He spoke loud enough for everyone to hear. He enumerated the reasons why he had volunteered, all of which seemed to make good sense. People looked at him and listened to him respectfully. I was no one to argue: I was out of tune with the world; I don't agree with the way it's run. He spoke about society. He made a lot of expansive gestures. He was all worked up, and the more he talked the more worked up he became. The others around him at the bar—five men and a woman—nodded in approval as he talked. The woman, a thin, nervous, dark-skinned creature, said that it was high time to have done with it. "Fortunately, there *are* still a few men," she shouted, turning toward the people who were busily eating, and who either appeared not to hear or made a good pretense of turning a deaf ear to her words. The others comprising the little group around the fighting man consisted of two workers in overalls and two middle-aged men who looked like white-collar employees. One of the latter had fought in the ranks of the revolution, in a country I seemed to remember was

Sardinia, while the other, a small, elderly man with a little white beard, had been an anarchist in his younger days, He was saying that the people shouldn't let themselves be taken in.

"In my day," he added, "in my day . . ."

"Yes," the man with the rifle declared, "it's now or never."

"We have to make them understand," added one of the workers.

"Things have to change," said the other worker, gulping down the rest of his drink.

The owner of the restaurant offered to pay for another round. The little knot at the bar accepted.

"It couldn't go on any longer," said the fighting man.

I agreed. I thought that things couldn't go on any longer, either.

"With guys like you . . ." one of the two white-collar workers said.

"We have to go all the way," the anarchist said. "Oh, if only I was your age!"

"A country of sluggards, that's what it is," the fighting man went on.

"We've had all we can take," said the woman.

"You can say that again," they all said in unison. "They're beneath contempt. . . ."

"Contempt is too good for them," one of them said.

"We have to settle this once and for all," said another.

"They'll be eliminated," the fighting man said. "Everyone will be better off because of it."

"You said it! Fair is fair!"

"We'll be fair," said the fighting man. "Fair and just. But they'll see that justice can be fair *and* harsh."

"All those who wallow in debauchery and injustice . . ."

". . . don't realize what they're doing."

"Oh, they do, many of them do!"

The fighting man turned toward our tables. I had the impression that I was the special target of his barbed remarks. He opened his mouth. I had no place to hide. Then I heard him say:

"Makes a man hungry as a lion, all that activity. I'm so starved I could eat a horse."

The old man with a white beard suggested that he join them for lunch, that he and the group of five at the bar all lunch together at the restaurant.

"I'd like to, I really would," he said, "but my wife is expecting me for lunch. I don't want her to worry. And besides, I need a little catnap. I'm due back on the barricades at three sharp."

He raised his hand in a militant salute and shouted:

"Down with the cops!"

"Down with the cops!" the others echoed. Then the fighting man headed toward the door, as the little group at the bar gazed after him.

Through the window, I could see him in the street. He looked fierce as he strode along. The group at the bar scattered; three left the restaurant, while the two others went over and sat down at one of the tables.

I felt uncomfortable. I have to do something, I said, not completely convinced by my own words.

"A brandy," I said to the waitress.

No, they're not really going to set my house on fire. I went on about my life. I had hired a new cleaning lady, a deaf-mute. It took her two hours every day to make the bed, sweep up, wash the glass I'd drunk from, open the windows to air out the apartment, then close the windows again. She also cleaned the curtains.

No, they won't set fire to the house. The battle still raged, but fairly far away. The people in the streets didn't seem overly concerned. The lady with her little dog still went out at the same time every day. The elderly retired couple, who lived in the little house across the way with the tiny garden, still took their daily stroll, each helping the other as they walked. The tall White Russian, the one with the lame leg, still wended his way home with his cane in one hand and a loaf of bread in the other. And then there was the fellow loaded down with groceries whom I always saw coming back from the market because his wife couldn't shop any longer; she must have been paralyzed. That's what the concierge told me, anyway. The concierge, believe it or not, was nicer to me now. She had grown used to me, which goes to show that people can grow used to anything.

Still, in the distance we could hear the crackling of gunfire, but faintly, faintly, you really had to bend your ear to hear it. Then after a time I forgot about it. But in the evening it seemed to grow louder.

In the morning I tended to get up rather late. I worked it so that I would leave just as the maid arrived. At lunch time. Every now and then I would think of the first waitress, what was her name again? Yvonne or Marie? Her replacement was very pleasant with me. Pleasant, but nothing more. Once in a while I would remember the other waitress, and for a sudden, painful moment wish she were back. But less and less. Still, I had to admit her departure had left a hole. One among many, one among many. Should

I screw up my courage and tell the other waitress how pleased I would be if she were to replace Yvonne? Or was it Marie?

On the avenue where the restaurant was located, two or three men carrying rifles could be seen. They mingled with the rest of the throng, so that they barely stood out from the others. In all probability, they were on their way to the square where the battle was raging. They were hardly distinguishable from the other idlers and dawdlers. No sign of them in my street, however, which was still as peaceful and provincial as ever. And yet it seemed as though the noise were growing closer. The people in the neighborhood didn't change their habits, though, still going out at the same time. The White Russian, the lady with the little dog, both cocked their heads, listening, but not very intently. I saw them from my window. They seemed to be slightly worried, or surprised, or perhaps it was only my projection that made me think so. Still, from my window on the fourth floor, I could see, beyond the street where the little houses stood, red flashes which doubtless came from the big square.

At the restaurant, both at lunch time and dinner, people still ate with their noses buried in their plates. I saw no further sign of the fighting man. I assumed it was because he was too busy. Perhaps he had been wounded or killed, or was in prison. Or perhaps he had thrown the whole thing over and gone away on a trip, perhaps he had said to himself that the game wasn't worth the candle, if that is the expression, and surely wasn't going to furnish us with the answers to our own existence. That was my opinion, too. Nothing could explain that mystery. People who spend their lives rushing hither and yon, not to mention to and fro, who claim to find the answers in action and incite others to follow their example and act too, are only evading the real issue, seeking to forget, the way I seek forgetfulness in alcohol.

One day about noon, as I was getting ready to go to the restaurant, I saw from my window a man all smeared with blood running down the street, with three policemen at his heels. At the corner, all four of them disappeared. This time, windows of the houses across the street shot up, as did those of my neighbors here in my own building. Heads appeared. I went downstairs. In the lobby, near the door, the concierge was holding forth with another concierge from a neighboring building, a wizened little old lady with white hair whom I had never seen before but about whom I had heard from various sources. Normally, she kept to her concierge's lair, but when she had heard the policemen shouting "Stop!" as they pursued the bloodied fellow, she had made an exception and ventured forth. The retired couple, the husband of the paralyzed wife, and the tall White Russian with his bread, formed a little circle around the two concierges. They had never seen such a thing on our street, which till now had always been a quiet, decent place to live.

"He's a thief," the man who was retired said.

"Maybe he's a revolutionary," said the White Russian.

"Oh, you, all you see is revolutions, no matter where you look," the retired man retorted. "You're not back in your own country, you know. This is France."

"You also had your revolutions," the White Russian responded.

"Sure, '89," said the retired man, "but that was a long

time ago. Here in our country we know what it leads to. We won't have another revolution here for a while, that I can assure you."

The man loaded down with groceries was of the opinion that something deeply disturbing was going on. "What do you think all those bright red flashes are that we can see? And what about the gunfire we've been hearing?"

The fact was, the sounds were louder; everyone could hear them now.

"It doesn't keep us from sleeping," the wife of the retired man put it.

To which the man loaded down with groceries added: "That's gunfire, and let no one be mistaken on that point. I'm a hunter, and I know gunfire when I hear it."

I broke into the conversation:

"And pray what do you think those red flashes in the distance are?"

The two concierges had never seen the sky glowing red.

"Because you both live on the ground floor," I told them. "Because the window of both your rooms looks out onto the courtyard!"

"All I can say is something seems fishy to me," said the second concierge.

"You can say that again!" my concierge chimed in, to no good purpose. But fortunately, the second concierge did not take up the offer.

"Don't worry," said the woman with the little dog, "nothing's going to happen. I know because my husband told me so."

The little group slowly dissolved. I went to lunch. As I turned the corner, I saw, on the sidewalk where the restaurant was, four men in single file. They were all carrying rifles and marching double-time in the direction of the big square. As they walked, they glanced nervously around. They looked as though they were ready to defend themselves at the drop of a hat. Defend themselves against whom? I asked myself. Two policemen were standing in their path. Neither moved. They acted as though they hadn't seen the men with rifles. Besides, it wasn't their job to arrest them. Their job was to direct traffic.

I opened the restaurant door and went in. I made my way to my table in the corner, near the window. I glanced around. People were talking, presumably exchanging opinions and information.

"Is something happening?" I asked the waitress as she brought a carafe of wine.

"Not that I know," she said. "I don't think so, I haven't read anything about it in the papers."

"And what about those bright red flashes that look as though they're coming from the big square?"

All the people on that peaceful street, that street where nothing ever happened, where nothing ever ought to happen, were all a little concerned. Most of the people who lived there were elderly. All they wanted was one thing: to live out their few remaining days in peace. To die peacefully. As for me, I was living in a state of catastrophe, independently of what was going on outside. Or rather, what was going on outside was going on in me. The outside was beginning to reflect the inside. Or vice versa. But it was only now that I was beginning to realize that fact.

I became aware of my malaise. It's true, I said to myself, since the day I was born I've always been ill at ease, uncomfortable. Why? What was it, what was wrong? So many people did manage to live and, until recently, seemed to get along all right, either reasonably happy or resigned. In any case, they didn't ask themselves too many questions. They weren't afraid of death, or rather they didn't dwell on the fact that one day they had to die. The problem with me was that I couldn't stop dwelling on that subject. Ever since my girl friend had left me, when I would wake up in the course of the night I would be panic-stricken: cold sweats, the fear that I was going to die at dawn. She was no longer there to say to me, "Come on now, take it easy and come to bed." Then I would remember that all I needed for the fear to vanish, as if by magic, was to hear her voice, or touch her, or feel her hand taking mine. Perhaps other people were prey to the same kind of panic. But their method of dealing with it was to act. They didn't like life, since they were revolting. Luckily, society was bad. What will they ever do if one day there is a society that is decent and fair? They perhaps will no longer be able to revolt against it, at which point the object of the anxiety will appear in all its stark nakedness, in all its horror. For me, the anxiety was there; no society could ever cure it. And anyway, all societies are bad. No matter how far back you went, back to the very mists of time, to time immemorial, was there ever one that worked? People kill one another in wars and revolutions. Send themselves as lambs to slaughter. People kill themselves by killing others. Or perhaps they're trying to kill death. And then all of a sudden I was engulfed by a wave of immeasurable sadness. I had put up with that situation since I had come into the world, but without being aware of it. It was the constant, "what's the use?" that had kept me from enjoying myself. A "what's the use?" that was not fully conscious. Now it was.

These were the thoughts that crossed my mind as I paced from one room of my apartment to another, from the bedroom to the hallway, the hallway to the living room, to the window through which you could see, more and more clearly, more and more distinctly, the bloody red flashes from the big square. I grew accustomed to the red glow; it no longer interested or preoccupied me, no longer amused me. I was too concerned with the interior panorama. My whole past unfolded in front of my eyes, a countryside of desolation and despair, a desert without an oasis. Rather, a chilly desert. From one end of the horizon to the other, that border where the cover met the ground, nothing: not even a flower. Dry earth at times, dust at others, and then at still other times, mud. Was it my fault? Was it only my fault? I hadn't known how to go about it. There could have been happy times, times when the gloom was pierced by a ray of joy. Is that true? Could there have been happiness? There might have been blinding light, instead of this dull gray, this bleak and dreary light. Could there have been light? Could there have been love? There could have been, there could have been. Think of all the missed opportunities! The women who had left me because I was incapable of love. My final chance had been with Yvonne. Or was it Marie? But there was love in me. In the vaults and prisons, in the dungeons of my soul. Locked up. The doors were locked and I didn't have the key. Alas, yes: all that was buried very deeply and distant. Yes, what a mess. A real mess. My sorrow was infinite. It was time to have done with it, once and for all. I had got off on the wrong foot. I hadn't got off at all. Yes, that was it: I'd missed all the starts. Now what could I do? Wait; wait in fear and despair. What? . . . If only I could start the whole thing over again. I would have liked to start again. But in order for something to start all over again, it first has to finish. Was there something to be hoped for? Was there something I could hope for? All was lost. Wasn't everything lost? My feeling was that all was lost.

And yet there were a lot of people around me. They wandered here and there, went about their business; they were transparent, they ate and slept, they said nothing to one another, or if they did speak it was to say nothing.

Were they sleepwalkers in life, for life? I saw that they were now waking up, that at least some of them were waking up. They were looking back with nostalgia to the good old days. They were doing something. Those people with rifles, that gunfire, that racing hither and yon. . . .

Since the beginning, there have been billions of human beings. Just counting our own time, there are some three billion of us. How did they all manage for centuries, for centuries and centuries? I thought of all those multitudes. Could it be that the unawareness was of infinite proportions?

The following day, or rather the morning of the day after, I awoke slightly later than usual. The doorbell was ringing. It must be the maid, the deaf-mute. I dried my hands and went to open the door for her. She looked terrified. She emitted all sorts of unintelligible sounds. I had grown used to her and had begun to be able to make out what she was saying. The sounds she was making now were expressions of fright. She kept pointing toward the window in the living room. I went over and opened it. Down below, a man was lying on the sidewalk, bathed in his own blood. The neighbors were standing in a circle around him. I closed the window, went downstairs, my face still half-covered with shaving cream.

I went over to where he was lying and pushed my way between the old retired couple. Both of them were shaking their heads.

"First time we've even seen anything like this," said the retired man.

His wife agreed with her husband's assessment.

"What is the world coming to?" the concierge said. "What times we're living through!"

"Lord, it's the son of the lady who lives down the block, you know, the one who lost her husband last year."

Just as these words were being uttered, the old concierge with white hair appeared, with the boy's mother in tow. The mother threw herself on her son's body.

"I told him he shouldn't get involved," she sobbed. "I told him to keep out of it, in no uncertain terms."

"Young people today," said the man loaded down with groceries, "have no sense of danger. . . . They don't even know what the word means."

"My poor boy," the mother was saying. "My poor, poor child."

The young man, who was no more than twenty or twenty-five, was unconscious. Short and dark, with curly, almost kinky hair, he looked frail. Fragile. His body was racked with convulsions.

"My God," people were saying, "how awful."

"Frightening."

"Terrifying."

Between sobs, the woman was moaning and crying out. "What have they done to him? He was so gentle. So kind and good."

As the police van arrived, the convulsions stopped. Four policemen emerged and savagely shoved the people aside. I got an elbow.

"Don't stand there, get moving," they said. "You heard me, get moving!"

"You're not traffic policemen," the White Russian exclaimed.

"Shut up and move along," the second policeman said to him, giving him a shove. "It's none of your business. It's not the likes of you who's going to teach me my job."

The policemen pushed, making the circle wider.

"What's she doing there!" the third agent shouted, pointing to the mother, who was sprawled over her son's corpse —for the youngster was now dead—clinging to him. The fourth policeman grabbed the mother, who did her best to fight him off, while the first policeman was busy writing something in a notebook. The woman was still sobbing and calling out:

"My child! Raymond, my little Raymond!"

"Come on, now, that's enough. That's not going to bring him back. You can see for yourself, he's not breathing any more."

The dead boy was wearing blue jeans and a blue shirt literally covered with red: his own blood. He had on a pair of slippers. One of the policeman rummaged around in the pockets of his blue jeans and came up with a switchblade.

Despite the mother's laments, two of the policemen picked up the body, to which his mother was still desperately clinging. They tried to pry her loose. They tossed the body into the police van. The two other policemen picked up the mother, who had collapsed on the sidewalk and was lying in the pool of her son's blood, still sobbing. Her hands were smeared with blood as they picked her up and tossed her into the van too.

"In you go. You can tell us how the whole thing happened."

The van containing the four policemen, the mother, and her dead son pulled away.

The pool of blood slowly widened on the sidewalk. Hypnotized, the people stood staring at it. The lady's little dog edged over and sniffed it, then licked it. The lady pulled him back by his leash. With one hand, I reached up and wiped away the shaving cream that was still on my face. Gesticulating broadly as they went, the people who had formed a little knot finally dispersed.

"You remember, he was the fellow who was running last week, the one whose face was covered with blood."

"No, that was somebody else. His enemy."

Only half-shaved, without my tie, I headed for the restaurant.

"That's life," I heard someone behind me saying, "you die."

"We all die, sooner or later."

I had an incredible thirst. A desire for alcohol. I turned the corner and went into the restaurant.

Something had changed, so much so that I wondered whether it was actually the same restaurant. Yes, it was the same. There were a lot of people sitting at the tables, but now I could see rifles leaning against the chairs, and the handles of revolvers protruding from people's pockets. Many of them were the same old customers, but others were new, faces I had never seen before. Almost all of them were armed, including the old-timers.

"What did you expect?" the waitress said when she saw my terrified expression. "People have to defend themselves."

"Wine," I managed. "Bring me some wine."

I took stock of the people who were there eating. I had some trouble recognizing the old customers, whom I had seen day in day out for so long. Their faces were different. There was something basically different about them. They were themselves, and yet they weren't. Some hitherto unknown aspect had revealed itself, another personality.

On every side people were talking, without paying the slightest attention to me. Snatches of their conversations drifted over to where I was sitting.

"The class struggle."

"The butcher of Red Square."

"The rich."

"The poor and downtrodden."

"A knife between his teeth."

"The proletariat."

"Primitive antirevolutionary."

"Dictatorship, yes, but with guarantees of freedom."

"Freely consented to."

"Tomorrow will be a better day. All our tomorrows."

"Bloody dawns."

"It'll be a new Monday-night Massacre!"

"Deeds have to be paid by blood, and blood alone."

"You have to admit they asked for it, with their stinking corruption."

"The workers are poor because they drink what they make. They're all alcoholics."

"Not to mention drugs."

"Collectivism."

"Individualism."

"Totalitarianism."

"The consumer society."

"Vampires of the people."

"They're all traitors, every last one of our leaders."

A tall, thin man who looked like an enraged tiger suddenly leapt to his feet and pounded his fist on the table with such vehemence that the silverware flew off in every direction. "And what about brotherhood!" he shouted. "Let's not forget brotherhood!"

His words were followed by a certain silence. People looked frightened. For a few seconds, they had interrupted their meals. The tall, thin man sat down. Then the discussions resumed.

"We've had it. Up to here!"

"Three-quarters of humanity live in poverty. If you can call that living. They're starving to death."

"We're the privileged ones."

"We're not privileged compared to those who are *really* privileged."

"Down with privileges."

"No more privileges."

"Something has to change."

"Men don't change. They stay the same."

"Revolutions come and go."

"Evolution or revolution?"

"Everything comes to an end. As everything has a beginning."

"It's attempting the impossible."

"Only the young people have the enthusiasm to. . . ."

"The young see more clearly than we do."

"The experience of maturity."

"The young are asses."

"The old are asses."

"There are young asses and old asses."

"Once an ass always an ass."

"We don't intend to stand by idly and let them take over."

"Revolution for the fun of it."

"We've had all we can take. Had it up to the gills, don't you see: Wake up—shape up. Work till you drop. Back to the brats. Sleep till you wake."

"Good times, don't you see, let the good times roll."

I was struck by the high level of the conversations, by all the fascinating observations being made by those people who up till now had struck me as being asleep. It seemed to me that something was stirring inside of me: the desire to stir. Perhaps some things were possible. Perhaps one could at least enlarge the area of the possible, expand the limits. There was such a crowd in the restaurant that day that the owner had to pitch in and help out, since the poor waitress had more than her hands full trying to keep the customers happy by herself. Despite all the hubbub, both the owner and waitress looked rather pleased, for business was booming. But some of the customers still felt the service was too slow. One man who was enormously fat, a kind of giant, snapped at the waitress, who, he claimed, wasn't moving fast enough. He said that they had no time to waste and that in half an hour they had to follow the funeral procession and see what was going on at the big square. The waitress responded in kind, that is tartly, saying she was doing her best and if he didn't like it he could pack up and leave.

"You're merchants," the fat man retorted. "Exploiters, that's what you are!"

"The exploitation of man by man," I heard from somewhere.

It was as though a tremor of anger had gone through the room again.

"I'm a worker," the waitress answered. "I earn my living by the sweat of my brow. All you do is talk talk talk. Words, empty words, that's all it is."

"Bitch!" the fat man flung at her. "Whore!"

That was more than I could take. Every ounce of heroism in me welled to the surface. It may not have amounted to much, but I did get to my feet:

"You ought to be ashamed of yourself," I said.

"You little bourgeois twerp!" the man said, red with anger. "I dare you to come over here and see what happens."

Foolishly, I did as he bid. When I was within range, he swung and hit me flush in the face with his fat fist. I staggered back and collapsed into my chair. Outraged, the waitress slapped the fat giant twice, two really good ones, and that sat him down, too. He sat there nursing his jaw. Then the waitress hurried over to me with a napkin and wiped away the blood that was flowing from my nose.

"Keep out of this whole thing," she said soothingly, "it's not something you should be involved in."

The incident passed almost unnoticed. But the nervous tension in the restaurant was clearly on the rise. As I was drinking a marc that the waitress had offered me, and at the same time still holding a handkerchief to my nose, bursts of gunfire could be heard in the street. Suddenly, as though someone had given an order, the people in the restaurant grabbed their rifles and jumped to their feet.

"The bill, the bill!" the owner and waitress screamed at them in desperation. Some of the diners tossed a few bank-notes in their face, with a deprecating: "Here's your lousy money!" Others simply shrugged their shoulders and re-fused to pay. Still others didn't even shrug their shoulders. In their rush for the door, they knocked things over and jostled one another. "Man your battle stations, citizens!" the people shouted. "We'll get 'em, we'll get the dirty krauts!" They rushed down the street, heading toward the big square. They joined a huge crowd already streaming past, which was armed with rifles or clubs. The street was filled with people, shouting, swearing, singing. I finally went out into the street. I hugged the wall to keep from being swept away. There were some shots. The street emptied. In the distance, you could still hear the cursing, and also the singing. On the pavement lay the bodies of two policemen and one old lady.

From the window of my living room I looked down at the street below. It was an unusually lively scene. Small groups of people were walking up and down the street, from one end to the other, arguing and talking as they walked. There were also some new faces: young people, quadragenarians, some bearded quinquagenarians. They were carrying rifles. Some of them had revolvers. Sometimes they pointed their guns skyward and shot into the air. People were emerging from little courtyards, from little gardens, and bidding good-bye to their families, their relatives. Where had they been keeping themselves up to now? I had never seen them in my life. They must have lived in little attics somewhere, way up under the eaves. Maybe they worked the night shift. Most of the time they were not alone, but accompanied by their wives, their mothers, their spouses, all of whom seemed to have handkerchiefs in their hands. They were doing their best to hold back the tears. I opened the window. The older people, who showed greater restraint than the women, were proffering words of encouragement to those departing. I could hear some of the words, which a gentle breeze wafted up to me, for the day was lovely, the sky was serene, indifferent.

"I know what it is to go off to war," said one wizened old man, "I fought in the war of '14."

"The Resistance," came from another somewhat younger.

"Yessiree, I've fought on the barricades," said a third. "I was there in '27, or was it '37? Not to mention '45. Or was it '35? Anyway, I was there!"

I hadn't realized there had been all that many barricades in our own land these past few decades. Maybe he was referring to somewhere else. Maybe the barricades he was referring to had been in Brazil. Or Spain. Maybe it had happened in the Belgian Congo, or in Palestine. At Odessa perhaps, or in China. Maybe in Ireland. The people who talked about being on all those barricades were probably mercenaries who volunteered their services to various foreign revolutions. Or perhaps they were foreign revolutionaries

The Hermit : **135**

who had sought refuge on our soil. The same situation had occurred in all countries. In some cases, the movements had ended successfully. In others, failure, which explained why it was necessary to start all over again, again and again. . . .

One of the militants raised his head and saw me in the window.

"What are you doing up there?" he shouted. "Come on down."

"I'm watching you," I shouted, "in utter amazement."

"Lazybones!" proffered another, his words obviously meant for me.

I closed my window and sank into my easy chair. "Maybe," I said to myself, not really believing my own words, "maybe I ought to go down and join them. I ought to do what everyone else is doing." But unfortunately, or fortunately, my weariness. . . . What would be the point of it? I asked myself, since we can't change the path of the sun? Since we can't postpone death. I think the reason they're all out there killing one another is because they weren't able to push death back. So in order to compensate they pushed and shoved one another, they went at one another tooth and nail. They went at one another tooth and nail because they couldn't explain the unexplainable. War, revolution, peace, boredom, worry, pleasure, sickness, health, love, women, squalling children. And that long road. That long road. The word "love" that had crossed my mind suddenly filled me with a feeling of great nostalgia. I realized that that could have helped me, might have replaced the explanation. To be madly in love. Actually, that was so unlikely, all that was so highly unlikely that it might appear enticing. I dreamed of a trip on a beautiful ship, the sea, the sky. Or the desert. Or else discovering deserted villages. In this world of ours, there still must be some places without any men. The image of a boundless sea, a calm desert, filled me with a feeling not unlike joy, not unlike hope. It still seemed possible for me to love the desert, to love the blue of the sea, the white of the ocean liners. To love people struck me as something else again. To not hate them was one thing. But to love them? Love these creatures who talked and moved and couldn't stay put for one minute, who made noise and made demands, who want and demand, who kick off? The notion was rather humorous. What can desire ultimately lead to? What can hate or killing, or simply conversation? We drag ourselves from one inexplicable to the next. To wait. Have confidence. Your heart filled to overflowing with love. There are people whose hearts are overflowing with love. There are people with hearts. There are hearts. No, I wasn't afraid. It wasn't fear that held me back, that stopped my élan before it had started. And what if I were afraid? To be afraid is human. "It's human, it's human," and I burst out laughing. The word "human" had made me laugh. There are no rules about fear, about what frightens some people while leaving others indifferent. When you think about it, it's rather funny. I was all wrought up about nothing. It's one more way of becoming all wrought up, but people like me, people who get worked up the way I do, never do anything about it. I shouldn't have suffered. And yet I did. I was all worked up about suffering. There was no point in not admitting it. In me there was nothing but turbulence, a turbulence which, for some strange reason, paralyzed me. . . . Thrusts and counterthrusts, contradictory and conflicting pressures. Once again I was only sorry I hadn't taken up philosophy. I might have learned something, I might have learned and understood a lot of things.

There was a knock on my door. It was the concierge, come to tell me that my cleaning lady, the deaf-mute, had been killed, by whom it remained unclear, either a rebel or a policeman. Whoever it was, he had ordered her to halt, and she had failed to respond to the order.

The concierge offered me her services, said she'd run errands for me if I liked, go shopping for me, clean the apartment.

"You need help, Monsieur," was her way of putting it, "and besides, you'll need a supply of tea, sugar, dried biscuits, dried meat, jam and jelly, coffee, and potatoes. There's plenty of room in your apartment. And there's space in the cellar, too. There's no telling whether we'll be able to go out."

As if to illustrate her words, the sound of gunfire grew louder. But in between there were moments of peace and quiet. She knew a greengrocer. The front of his store was all boarded up, but if you knew the way you could go in through the back. Needless to say, his prices were on the high side.

I said that I was in total agreement, naturally. And yet the thought of not going back to the restaurant any more distressed me no end. I was going to miss it. I was completely lacking in imagination. How could I have failed so totally to foresee what was coming? At the first alarm, the first little signs of trouble, why hadn't I turned tail and departed with whatever money I still had? Now, you could be sure, it was going to be worth less and less, what with all the upheavals and changes that would be occurring. I could have taken an exotic express train, that one they call "the blue train," or a silver plane streaking through the sky. Or a ship. Or simply a car with a chauffeur. Right now I could be strolling peacefully through some gleaming, sun-filled city, walking down streets whose houses were all painted pink. I could have been climbing leaning towers, visiting museums in some foreign country famous for its art. All alone. I would have been bored. I should have suggested such a trip to Yvonne. Unless her name was Marie. Maybe that's what she was waiting for: trips, voyages. . . . Oh, I was better off here where I was, here in this midst of all this chaos and confusion. Never a dull moment.

I couldn't bear it any longer. I took advantage of a lull in the fighting to go outside.

"Be quick about it," the concierge had shouted after me. "They've stopped for lunch, but as soon as the lunch hour is over they'll start in again. They're on our street now, and they shoot at anything that moves. Don't cross the street. Just go as far as your little restaurant, and come straight back. Hurry!"

I went toward the restaurant, at a slightly faster pace than usual, turned the corner into the avenue, and went into the restaurant, which fortunately was open.

"Hurry up and come inside," the waitress shouted at me. "We may still be open tomorrow, but the day after I doubt it."

I sat down at my usual table. The windows had large, gaping holes in them, with long cracks in those still generally intact.

"Yes," said the waitress, "what happened was, the people in the restaurant fired out at the people in the street, and the people outside fired in at our customers. Today's special is animal snout with mustard sauce."

"Are you going away somewhere?"

"The owner didn't want to join the leadership of the revolution. He's not as young as he used to be. And what was more, he wasn't sure the revolutionaries were going to win. So they have it in for him."

"If they were real revolutionaries," said the owner, who appeared out of nowhere, "I might have given them a helping hand. But actually, they're reactionaries."

"And what about the others, their opponents?"

"They're reactionaries, too. They're both bands of reactionaries. One side is being backed—and financed—by the Lapps, the other by the Turks."

Armed soldiers were marching past the restaurant window. Some of the soldiers shook their fists at us. Others scowled. Still others struck the windows, and might have broken them. The waitress took my plate and silverware and moved them to the middle of the room.

"Just look at them," said the owner, "you ever seen such Ottoman heads in your life?"

"Don't be racist," I said. Then I shut up, choking back my saliva.

"*I'm* a racist," the waitress said, "because I love all races. No one foreign is alien to me."

"There's no such thing as races," the owner said.

"In that case, I don't love anyone," the waitress responded, "except for the yellow race."

"There aren't any races," the owner said.

"The yellow people then," the waitress said.

"The yellows are all traitors," the owner said. "When I used to work in the factory, they were always the strikebreakers. In any case, you're not going to see me getting mixed up in this suburban revolution. We're going to move in to the center of town, where things are peaceful."

Someone came into the restaurant. Derby hat, spats, and a mustache.

"I crossed the rebel camps to reach your section of town. I wanted to see whether they'd burned down my business. It's true what you say: in the center of town, on the far side of the big square, things are calm, half a mile or so from here. Stretches of calm. The streets are calm. Much less traffic, fewer people coming and going in the streets. Over there people sit home, glued to their television sets. They watch the revolution on TV. And farther still, over in the western suburbs, the leaves have come out on the trees. Beyond are the broad highways, that stretch as far as the eye can see, farther even, on and on. . . . And then there's the countryside. Apple trees in bloom. And the beautiful river flowing to the sea. And at the shore there are beaches, enormous beaches. And beyond the beaches lies the ocean. Now, at this time of year, the ocean is calm, as calm as the lakes nestled high in the mountain peaks.

"And then there are the islands. Full of lush vegetation. Eternal springtime. Naked women. We're in a prison, to be sure, but the prison is large and beautiful, with parks and gardens. In the gardens, the guards are good-natured and pleasant. They smile at you, and none carries any night stick. And in the islands there aren't even any guards, or if there are they remain in hiding, out of sight in the woods, fast asleep."

Suddenly I saw the universe in all its magnitude and splendor, in all its vast variety. In this world there were paths, there were mountains, there were fields and meadows, a kindly sky, men who practiced brotherly love. There are countries which welcome foreigners with open arms and treat them kindly. They are given food to eat and something to quench their thirst; they live in houses without any roof because there it never rains. The stars are so low it seems you can reach out and touch them. Like clusters of fruit.

I had some money in a bank located in the center of town. I made up my mind to go over and retrieve it. Someone loaned me a helmet. I didn't want a rifle. There were some bulletproof vests available at what had been the hosiery shop before it had been taken over by the weapons' dealer, but their sale was restricted to the fighting men. I headed off in the direction of the big square, intending to cross it and walk from there to the center of the city, to the peaceful stretches. The avenue was blocked off by a barricade. I waved a white handkerchief. It was perforated by a bullet. I ran toward the other end of the street, where there once had been big factories and tall smokestacks which had been demolished, forming an impassable wall of stone and brick in the middle of the pavement. Impossible to scale the wall, but also impossible to skirt it right or left. To the right was a fortified area manned by the rebels, whose sentinels fired on anyone who dared come near, and who sometimes simply fired a few blasts at random for the fun of it. To the left lay the police encampment, and the police were arresting anyone and everyone. I was obliged to beat a fast retreat, and found myself caught up in the surging crowd. I wove my way among the throngs until I reached my restaurant. It was just closing. I saw the waitress stooping down to slip out from under the iron screen that had already been lowered three-quarters of the way.

"Tell Yvonne to wait for me," I shouted at her.

"I'm not in touch with her any more," she answered. "I haven't seen her for over a year."

"Do you know whether she's married or not? Does she have any children?"

"Four," was the waitress' last word before she disappeared.

How long had it been since Yvonne had left me? Had it been months? Or years? Time goes by so fast. I had heard a number of people comment on that fact. It wasn't the first time that I had felt how true it was. Time goes by, time has gone by, and here I am on the edge of the abyss.

I turned the corner of the street, heading for my house. But it was no easy matter to make it home. A barricade had been built on the near end of the street, that is the end closest to the restaurant. I hurried past, saying that I was a resident of the neighborhood.

"You live on this street," they said to me, "and you don't know the password? Well, go along anyway."

I walked down the street and saw that at the far end they were also building a barricade.

My house was located near the middle of the block. When I reached my door, I could see the flag on the barricade at the far end. It was the same flag as the one on the barricade at the near end. A green field bearing a crescent moon and a sheaf of wheat.

"But," I cried in surprise, "it's the same flag!"

The old man from the house across the street came over to where I was standing.

"Go and tell them. They both belong to the same party. They're slaughtering each other."

"They both have field glasses. They must know exactly

what they're doing. I suspect two rival leaders of the same group are having it out."

Scarcely had I said these words than a burst of gunfire erupted from both ends of the street. We were trapped in the crossfire. My hat was pierced by a bullet, but just above the headband. The old man crumpled, shouting, "Long live . . ." A stream of blood prevented me from learning what it was or who it was the old man would have liked to see live long. The old man's wife emerged from the house across the street. Seeing her husband lying on the ground, she gave a blood-curdling scream, naturally. She shook her fist at me. "It's all your fault," she yelled, "dirty bourgeois!"

The gunfire was growing more and more intense. I ducked into my entranceway without giving the old lady or the old man another thought. In the lobby, I threw down my hat in anger: "I'm through with hats," I shouted. "I'll never wear another hat!"

"Don't stand there so close to the door," the concierge admonished. "Hurry on upstairs. I've laid in a good supply of food. You have everything you need for months."

"You didn't forget the . . ."

"I didn't forget anything. I thought about what you're thinking of. You have enough to last you for months, maybe even years. Since you like being alone anyway, you'll be happy up there in your little nest. Assuming they don't cut off the electricity, and the toilet still flushes."

I climbed up to the fourth floor, and opened my door. She had not been exaggerating: there was everything I would need. Everything. The whole apartment was filled with bottles, wine from various parts of the country: Bordeaux, Burgundy, Savoy, Alsace, and Touraine. The hallway was filled with mineral waters of one kind and another, from one end to the other. Chock-full. And bags filled with food. The rats and mice would certainly never make it up this high. But just in case, I had in mind to set up barricades against them at every door and window. And at the pipes. I had a stock of poison for rodents. And even a revolver. There was so much food I could scarcely make it to the windows, which was just as well, for stray bullets often came crashing through them. Still, I would edge to one of the windows and peek out of one corner at the street below. I saw that from the barricades at both ends of the street men were streaming, charging one another's positions. Shots, a growing uproar, shouts of rage, screams of the wounded, death rattles, medics racing to and fro. There was no end to it. Bodies were strewn all over the street. The fighting raged for three days, or four. The barricades were being constantly replenished with new troops, at regular intervals, once in the morning and again in the evening, to take the places of those who had fallen. And still the street resounded with moans and screams, and the militant songs, and the insults hurled back and forth. The people who lived on the street who had not taken part in the battle all seemed to be having a good time. In spite of the danger, they kept their windows wide open, watching the proceedings. Every now and then one of them paid the supreme penalty. A stray bullet would take them unawares. Not always stray, either. Sometimes the fighters in the street below would lose patience and fire up at the spectators. Since they were having a wild time anyway, what the hell: what was one spectator more or less? Not that you could blame them. After all, they were only human. The people who were struck by the bullets simply disappeared inside their houses. Sometimes, though, they fell the other way, that is out the window: plop! Right in the middle of the pavement, believe it or not! Sometimes an effort was made to gather the bodies of these innocent victims, both camps fighting furiously to claim possession. That way, each side could accuse the other of being a gang of cutthroats and murderers of the elderly, and of women and children. To tell the truth, I didn't find the whole thing especially amusing. I was gorged with all that blood, glutted with so many corpses.

"Still," I said to myself, "there's no denying all this will surely inspire some lovely graphics—full-color pictures of soldiers in action for future generations."

I decided that I had waited long enough. Too long. I had had more than my fill of these bloody spectacles, these theatrical or cinematographic ruins, these events which would provide subject matter for a whole generation of writers, for tens of thousands of books. Besides, it still was far from over. It would doubtless go on for years and years, with patches of hope in the distance like a tiny bit of blue among the clouds. The flames and heavy smoke from the endless fires prevented me from seeing the starry sky of the cosmic prison. What Oriental legend was it, unless it was Arabian, that told how there lay, beyond the vault of heaven, beyond the cosmic cover, a shining light. The stars, so the legend goes, are really the holes through which this blinding light streams.

I decided to barricade myself in the apartment and let nobody in.

I no longer had any reason to go out. The water, the heating, gas, and electricity were working to perfection. Why? Because all those services came to us through huge conduits which had been laid so far underground that neither the rebels nor the antirebels had the means or ability to dig down far enough to blow them up. Not that mass destruction was not taking place all around: factories, garages, administration buildings were being destroyed throughout the neighborhood. But since all the combatants had to pause for breath from time to time, and go on an occasional leave, they did spare a few houses, a few streets, mine in particular, because many of them lived in the rooms under the eaves in the houses across the way, or because their relatives lived in the neighborhood, and when they went on leave they would come to pay them a visit. These houses also served as depots for their food and clothing, and their munitions. Once in a great while one of the houses would explode, but it was the exception rather than the rule.

No munitions at all were stored in our house, and no one who lived there was in any way related to any of the combatants. From time to time one of the fighters would appear in the building, brought there by our sole militant, the lady with the little dog whose husband, quite coincidentally, had just died. They all had long hair and long beards. After a certain amount of time had elapsed following the death of her husband, the lady with the little dog brought home with her one of the rebels who, though he still had a beard, had his head completely shaved, which must have meant that he belonged to the opposite camp from those with long hair. So that was it: she was playing fast and loose. Occasionally, the two enemy rebels would run into each other at the lady's house, but probably bearing in mind that our house was thought of as a no man's land, or neutral territory, they opted for wisdom instead of valor and worked out a *ménage-à-trois*.

I thought of these pipes and underground cables which brought us our heat and light from the center of town. I thought about my former colleagues from the office, too, and how much fun they must be having at my expense! Here I was imprisoned in this dangerous suburb, in which anger and madness, blood and death had been raging all this time. So long, in fact, had the battle been going on in our once fair suburb that they in the center of town would have had plenty of time to build new parks with graceful lawns. The trees there were surely taller than I remembered them, and everything must be beautiful and pleasant.

For some time now my windows had been the target of snipers. Had they spotted me as a dangerous neutralist? The fact was, I didn't understand the first thing about why they were fighting. But I had to assume there was indeed a reason.

One day, after I had already long since grown used to the noise and danger, I was reading, or more correctly rereading, an old newspaper that dated back to before the "events," as we referred to them, when I got up, having an urge to urinate. While I was out of the room, I had heard the sound of breaking glass, and when I came back fully intending to lie down again on the sofa, I saw a magnificent splinter of a shell right in the spot where my buttocks were wont to perch. I wanted to make sure that such an accident would not recur. I decided that the best way was to give the impression that my apartment was deserted. I stuffed two fat mattresses in the windows, and added some cushions for good measure. They were so well plugged that not a ray of light seeped through.

I decided to move into the room in the back, whose window looked out onto the courtyard. It was an inside yard, so quiet you could hear a pin drop. The room was quite light, because I lived on the fourth floor, and the room faced south. At times, it was even sunny. Well, a ray now and then, sometimes several. The younger children had been sent away, either to the country or to boarding schools in the center of town. Their parents had left with them. Children thirteen and older, the concierge had told me, had signed up on one side or the other. It was not just idle gossip; she showed me a rebel paper which confirmed what she said. The paper, I learned, had been found in the lobby. These children, the story went, had gone off to form, on the one hand, a military or paramilitary unit known as the "Cohort of Urban Ragamuffins," and, on the other, a group called the "New Wilson Legion." There was also a third group, the "Suburban Boy Scouts." Their jobs were to gather and care for the wounded on both sides, and to scrounge or steal chickens and other foodstuffs meant for the fighters from both camps, assuming there were only two, or all three or four, assuming there were more. In return for the food they appropriated, they gave coupons to those from whom they took it.

From my fourth-story window I could see that the courtyard of the house was already filled with a pile of garbage, a little hillock on which grass was already growing, and a scattering of tiny trees in flower. So I could toss my leftovers into the courtyard, confident in the knowledge that it would be metamorphosed into green plants, flowers, and grass. My last link to the outside world, that world of fire and gunpowder which surrounded me on all sides, was the concierge. And even that link was tenuous: the hallway was so chock-full of supplies and bottles that she could hardly get through, so that I made a little passage for her by pushing the bags and bottles back against both walls. I moved my bed into the former storeroom. It was an oasis, a tiny Switzerland of peace and quiet. In all likelihood, it would be some time before I could leave my retreat, but meanwhile I had what I needed to hold out. The calm was reassuring, as was the fact that no one was lurking behind the silent windows. I knew that I would enjoy living here, and that I would have plenty of time to dream, and to drink all the alcohol my heart desired.

Time went by. Months went by. Years maybe. Every now and then the concierge brought me up some colored graphics depicting soldiers of the revolution, with their rifles and beards and caps. Or else beardless and capless. The "events" had already become history. One of the pictures portrayed Bara's death: his body crisscrossed with bayonet wounds, he was in the act of falling. Another picture showed one of the ragamuffins, also toppling, his arm raised to the sky. On the opposite side of the picture the bad guys were still firing at him. The bad guys were dressed in greenish uniforms.

One day the concierge told me that they had finally blown up some of the houses on our street. So that's what all those tremors had been. I cocked my ear, but for the life of me all I could hear was the faint sound of shooting somewhere in the distance.

"Actually," the concierge said to me, "the only fighting going on now is on the big square."

Even there, it was far less ferocious than before. Between fusillades, or during momentary periods of calm, people went to the races. I was interested to find out what had become of my restaurant.

"It's gone, Monsieur," the concierge said, "all those houses are gone. Nothing but rubble."

Our house, and two or three houses adjacent to it, formed a tiny island in a sea of ruins: they were the only ones left standing. There were very few people left in our street, either. The retired couple, the White Russian, and the lady with the little dog, were about the only ones left. All the others were dead. Not all of them had been victims of the civil war, to be sure; some had died of old age, of a heart attack, of other illnesses.

"But it will all be rebuilt," the concierge assured me. "It'll provide people with work. Do you have any idea how much a square foot of land is worth on this street today? Do you?"

The concierge died, too. Her daughter took her place. It was quite some time before I noticed the change, however, because provisions were dropped off for me, and empty tin cans picked up, without my ever seeing anyone. It was rare that I had any outside contact. And then there came a time when I saw no one at all.

My room was bright. Filled with sunshine. I made it a strict rule with myself to take a trip to the bathroom, wash up, and shave every day. On cloudy days, however, I still washed but I didn't shave. After I had finished, I made my way along the tiny path that I had created between the piles of food and stacks of bottles, and lay down again. I made my bed, swept up a bit. I opened the door to my room to put out the dirty linen and pick up the clean. All that took a great deal of time and effort, and made me tired enough to feel fully justified in once again taking to my bed, from which I could see the sky or the ceiling. I was waiting. For what I didn't know. But an active, pulsing wait. I tried to read signs from heaven, and when cottony clouds would pass by, mixing with the blue, I tried to fathom what it might mean. I wasn't unhappy the way I once had been. Was it age that had made me wiser, or had age merely blunted the forces that had stirred and struggled within me? I don't want to give the mistaken impression that I was happy, either. Here is how things stacked up. Within the confines of the great, universal prison, I had made for myself a smaller prison, a prison made to order. I had carved out for myself a little niche in which I could live. It was tiny, I had no doubt about that point. But at least it was made to measure, to my measure. A little niche in a prison that kept me from seeing the prison. A prison without work? Was I bored? Was I resigned? Tired, no doubt. But I did have the possibility to lie down whenever I wanted, however I wanted. I spent hours, even days, stretched out on my bed. Except for that wait, that feeling of great expectation, no effort was required of me, none at all. As I looked up at the sky, I always tried to see beyond it. Does "I" exist? "I" was here, nonetheless, between two infinities, the large and the small. What was I? On the one hand, a speck. On the other, a conglomerate of galaxies; I was billions of centuries for cosmic systems. I was billions and billions of miles for people I didn't even know, for billions of people who consorted within me, who became indignant and revolted, who fought one another, loved one another, who loathed one another. Yes, all that was in me.

My house, and the two or three adjacent to it, were now a tiny island surrounded by a vast building project. They were rebuilding what had been demolished. The reason they demolish is so that they can rebuild. And the reason they rebuild is so that they can demolish. The intervening walls of two or three houses protected me from the noises of reconstruction. Anyway, I had my own method for dealing with the problem. I didn't try to fight the noises. I didn't block my ears, didn't lose my temper, didn't rant and rave. No, what I did was listen as attentively as possible to the noise. It was a kind of music. Instead of getting on my nerves, it tended to relax me.

There were a number of beautiful days. Perhaps that was because I lived in the southern suburbs where it was warmer and sunnier than in the northern suburbs. One day, a short while before noon, as I was looking up at the blue sky above the rooftops as was my wont, I saw a slit appear, a slight crack which silently spread from one end of the azure vault to the other. The crack was luminous, a light stronger than the light of day, or—how can I describe it?—a bluer blue than the blue of the sky. I was hoping for something. The construction noises went on as before, as if nothing were happening. Needless to say, not everyone has the time or the bent for sky-watching, especially when you do it properly, that is attentively. But people don't lift their eyes, probably because their work and worries don't leave them any time for it. I continued to gaze upon that lizard in the sky. My eyes were smarting, but still I refused to look away. Slowly but surely, the luminous ray, the light within the light disappeared, the same way it had appeared, without leaving a trace. The streak reappeared at night among the stars, broader than it had been during the day. It was like a flash of lightning frozen from one end of the horizon to the other. The stars in the vicinity of the cleft grew pale, and seemed to go out. And yet it was from one of these stars, one of these distant points of light, that this greater light, as bright as the light of two suns, had begun.

Again, happiness welled up within me. I took it for a promise and not a menace. As day dawned, the streak withdrew from the sky. Dawn itself seemed gray by comparison.

Roughly at eight o'clock, the young concierge brought me my coffee. No, she wasn't in the habit of looking up over the rooftops. She hadn't noticed a thing. In the first place, she spent her nights sleeping. During the day she was too busy. She had work to do. She would look up at the sky on Sunday. What was more, no one in the building, including the workers who lived there, a number of whom she counted among her friends and whom she had run into on her way to fetch some bread that morning, not to mention the baker herself, had said anything to her about it. The only one who had was me. I said to her that between now and Sunday the phenomenon might well not recur.

"I don't spend all my time daydreaming," she said spitefully.

"I give you my word," I added, "I really saw it."

"And I tell you that no one I know mentioned a word about it to me."

She asked me to make out a check for her so that she could go do the shopping. She also informed me that the new tenants in the building had demanded that the owners install a new elevator, and I would have to pitch in and contribute my fair share—which came to a considerable sum. She stressed how much I would benefit from the new elevator if only I would get up and venture outside once in a while. My living like a hermit this way made no sense. There was no longer any danger. Oh, once in a great while one did hear a few explosions, and the distant sound of bombs bursting in air. They had paid for it dearly, but for the time being the neighborhood was quiet. The revolution had moved northward, off toward the center of town and the northern suburbs.

"It's about time they had a taste of it. We've had more than our share."

All that day and for the next several days after, and the following Sunday, too, I leaned out the window looking up beyond the rooftops at the sky, hoping the phenomenon would repeat itself. For several Sundays, several weeks. Nothing further was taking place up there in the higher regions.

I once again grew accustomed to the ordinary light of day. And I grew bored. I even entertained the idea of leaving the apartment and going outside. In all likelihood, they would have reconstructed a new restaurant on the site of the old one. I went through a difficult and uncomfortable period. I made my way gingerly the length of the hallway, still flanked on both sides by my provisions, reached the door, and opened it. I went downstairs, astonished at how easy it was. I walked past the concierge's room. No one was there. The old concierge never used to go out. She stayed put in her own little lair. Other times, other customs. I took one step, a second, along the sidewalk. I didn't recognize any of the houses. They were all brand new; big, tall buildings that all looked alike. A new street intersected ours, built on the site of some houses that had been destroyed. The new street made the walk to the avenue shorter. The little houses, with their little yards or gardens, were no longer there. I didn't know any of the new neighbors. She was right: in the distance I could hear the bombs bursting, presumably in air. I pushed on till I reached the restaurant.

The old owner had come back and reoccupied the old premises. The government for or against which he had fought had renovated the old place and set him back up in business there. He had a limp, and I was struck at how old he had grown. But then I suppose I had aged, too, for he didn't recognize me. The clientele had changed as well. The customers were all young, some of whom were playing guitars, while others were drinking non-alcoholic beverages, of all things. All of them seemed to be enjoying themselves immensely. They were laughing loudly. Several of them were sitting with their chairs tilted back, with their feet up on the table. The world has grown young, I said to myself, and I've grown old. They'll grow old, too. Then, addressing the owner:

"You remember me," I said, "I'm the fellow who used to eat here at the same table every day, over there at that formica table where all the young people are."

"Oh, yes, yes, I seem to remember," the old man said. "No, I don't have any waitress any more. Oh, she must have grown children by now. Grandchildren maybe. Come, let me offer you a drink. It won't be long now before I retire. And what about you? How's your work going?"

"You must remember, I retired while I was still quite young. I've been retired for a long time."

"You are the lucky one! So you must be having a good life. Still, you look a little seedy to me, if you must know. Oh, don't give it another thought; it happens to the best of us. Maybe if you'd worked, though, you wouldn't have gone down hill so fast. Stagnation, that's the danger when you retire: you have to cast around and find something to keep you busy. Trade in one job for another, that sort of thing.

Recycle yourself, as they say today. Do you remember the civil war, and the barricades? Ah, let me tell you, those were the days. They don't make them like that any more. Why, would you believe it if I told you that shots were exchanged right here, in this room."

"I know, I remember very well, since I was right here."

"So you were, so you were, I'd forgotten for a moment. And that extraordinary right hook to the face you received. That's what life is all about, eh? Luckily, there's still plenty of good wine around," pouring another round at the bar. "As long as there are bars to pour on, there will always be wine to pour. But the cheese, have you noticed the difference? No comparison with what it used to be in our day. Can't find a decent cheese to save your life. Mass produce it, that's what they do. It's easier. The youth don't want to work; they're lazy. Why, a shot could go off right outside and they'd sit there on their fat buttocks, not moving a muscle. No, the fact is they'd move all right. Can't ever figure what's going on in people's minds."

"How true, how true! There's an aggressive turn in all of us, and no telling when it might show up."

As I left, the young people turned and watched me go. I knew they were poking fun at me, winking and jabbing their elbows in one another's rib cages. No doubt because I was dressed in the old style. Or because I belonged to another world. Perhaps a world that was already dead and gone. Were there still any bourgeois left? Was I a bourgeois? And what if I weren't, but wasn't anything else, either?

I hurried home as fast as I could. Clutching my aching back, I went up the stairs, opened my door, locked it behind me, and, without so much as a glance at the living room, settled back down in my room.

Little by little the noises came back. They struck me as being far away. And yet I was able to tell them apart: drilling machines, air hammers, cement mixers, cranes. Songs, too, the voices of workers. Since the whole thing was so deafening, I began to think that I had grown hard of hearing. A new world was a-building, a new world, they must be saying to themselves. The mere thought wore me out.

I must have irritated the concierge no end, what with all the extra work I put her to: bringing my meals up three times a day, picking up my dirty laundry and depositing my clean, plus all the other errands she had to run. She asked me for a raise.

"Money's not worth what it used to be," she told me. "You have no idea how prices have gone up."

I agreed to her demands. Then I was hit with a feeling of near-panic. Was I going to have to go out and look for a job? The thought was more than I could bear. And then there was the other thought, even worse, of whether I was still capable of doing anything. It took me a long time to pull myself together, but I finally did write to my lawyer and to the bank. Their replies were reassuring. My money was turning over. My income had increased roughly in proportion to the rise in the cost of living. Still, one couldn't be too careful, so I decided to cut out smoking. I couldn't cut out alcohol, but even there I made a sizable reduction in my daily ration. As for meat, only twice a week. I ate less in general. The concierge told me about a people's restaurant that had opened up in the neighborhood, where they sold hot meals you could take out. I preferred that to canned goods, or the stew that the concierge cooked up for me. Besides, I wanted to spare her as much as possible, take less of her time. She also had to look after her sister's babies, since her sister had married and now worked on one of the construction crews. Her husband was ill, and social security was at best only a fraction of what they needed to keep body and soul together.

I did my best to placate the concierge, who scolded and grumbled, slammed my door, laughed in my face. I even made an effort to strike up a conversation with her, but my forced gaiety and little jokes didn't seem to be her cup of tea. I have a suspicion that the way I lived, the way I acted, rarely if ever going out, must have struck her as odd. She made a number of discreet allusions to my inactivity, then stopped pussyfooting around:

"I say what I think," she said, "I'm not one for mincing words, mind you, I tell people exactly what's on my mind!"

It was for her that I made an effort in the morning to wash and shave and make myself more or less presentable, so as not to offend her, to try to placate her at least a little. My hair was graying at the temples. How long had it been since I. . . ? According to her, I had no right to be retired in the first place. Not at my age, anyway, "especially after the life you've led, never doing a thing. What good are you anyway?" What good was it working for someone who was no good? I preferred not to go into that question. "In any event," she concluded, "you'll have to be moving soon. They're going to tear down this house soon, this last little island of old houses. They're going to put up something modern."

"Which will also grow old, like everything else. You don't even have time to catch your breath."

She didn't answer, simply shrugged her shoulders. Tear down my house soon? The idea sent a little tremor through me. I set my mind at ease. Hadn't I heard that same threat before? It will probably be years before they do anything. Furthermore, I could object to the house being torn down. I owned the apartment, after all. Still, they would raise the issue of public interest. They could force me. Oh, but it would take time.

I wondered what had become of the others? My old colleagues at the office, my old girl friends? Dead, or mothers-in-law. Grandmothers maybe. What if I went to pay them a visit one of these days? Was the civil war still raging in the center of the city where they were located? Should I try to find out?

When I thought of the past I had a feeling not unlike that of sadness or nostalgia. Yes, I missed the old bistro, drinks with the owner of the place, drinks with my old pal, what was his name? Jacques? Jacques, I think. . . . No, that wasn't it, Jacques was Lucienne's husband. Wasn't his name Pierre? Pierre what? His last name began with a B. . . . With a B? Something like Bouille. As for the name of the boss, for the life of me I couldn't remember it, or even what letter it started with. I haven't much of a memory. And yet it hadn't been all that long. It hadn't been all that long. My youth. The old streets, the old houses of the city, it's a beautiful city. It used to be beautiful on Sundays, when I would sit on the café terrace, or at the brasserie, and watch the world go by. Sundays. The hotel. You opened your window and looked out at the street literally swarming with people. That was before the war. And then there had been the waitress, Yvonne. She was the one I regretted the most. Oh, the long, lost days that come no more! I was philosophizing. What else was there? Rain, sunshine, the movies. I went to the movies, but only rarely. So many interesting films. Too late. Think of all the things I would have learned. I wouldn't have learned anything. What is there to learn? Memory, memory: what do you want from me? More than anything else there had been the lights, at night, the lights of the city. More than anything else there had been the gray days, the gray houses, the gray people. There had also been, but only once, a shining white road. A day that had been especially bright. That hadn't been in the city. Yes, I had taken a trip. An automobile trip with Lucienne. Had it been with Lucienne? I had been amazed by the variety of colors in the countryside, the red poppies in that wheat field. We had climbed out of the car, we had walked for a few hundred yards down a sunken road, with up ahead the sunshine playing among the green leaves. We had emerged into that wheat field.

And then there were also the memories I had heard from others. My friend at the office, what was his name again? I ought to remember it. Anyway, he had once taken a long bus trip through Belgium. He had taken it a long time back, that is long before he had told me about it, when he was still quite young. It had been a fun trip, with everyone talking and laughing and drinking wine that they had taken from their luggage. When they had reached the border, policemen had come onto the bus and asked them for their passports. Then they had gone on their merry way. Ponds, little towns, houses built of red brick. And then they had reached Brussels, some place near the train station, where it had started to pour, but really pour! They had left the bus and dashed across the street to a long, narrow bar with painted tables. And there they had drunk beer, that special Belgian beer they call "gueuse," you know the kind. They had drunk a barrel of it, and they had had a ball. It had all been great fun. And after that they had gone on to Antwerp. Down near the port the houses had pointed roofs, not at all the way they're built in our country. There were women in the windows. It was a dangerous area. Fights were frequent, though none had broken out during their visit, which was a shame. They would have enjoyed seeing a good old free-for-all. It wasn't dangerous, not as though they had been alone there. And anyway, there were policemen on every street corner, keeping a careful watch. Belgian policemen.

I also remembered that girl who had died when she was nineteen. Her coffin was covered with flowers and wreaths. Flowers of every color of the rainbow. I wanted to smell them. After I did, I lost my sense of smell. Apparently that can happen to someone who smells the flowers of a person who has died. For a long time all I could smell were the foul odors. Later on my sense of smell returned, at least partially. When I was small I was a regular sniffer, renowned for my sense of smell. They used to blindfold me, and I could identify my school chums simply from the smell of their overcoats. It never came back a hundred percent.

It's not true: everything wasn't gray. And yet the memories that shine are rare indeed, maybe one or two, no more; all the rest is dark and dirty streets at night. Streets glistening and wet.

The image of my mother also came back to haunt me. Thin, with her gray hair, her gray dress, her gray face, and her ambition for me to "make it." Does anybody ever "make it"? And then the office, the time cards, the political discussions with my office companion, the arguments too, making up by the time we left the office at dusk, the gray hour, to have a drink together. So many blanks, blank because I drank too much alcohol, the purpose of which was to obliterate the images. Every now and then a vague glimmer, a half-glimmer in the shadow-curtains. There had also been revolutions, civil wars, the fist flush in my face. And then there had been things going on around me, without me. While I may not have been directly involved, I was none-theless interested. There had been corpses. There had been revolutionary marches, men beside themselves with anger. So angry they couldn't contain themselves. And the young man on the sidewalk surrounded by the neighbors who lived on the block that had changed so much. Those old folks, those retired people, so thin and frail: had they ever really existed? It was as though it never had existed. And what about the little old man with his white mus-tache? Did he also have a beard? Or a goatee? Or only a mustache? Before the revolution, what a pleasant street this had been, so quiet and peaceful, with all these old people, that Russian who limped. I hadn't loved him enough. In my mind's eye I ran through all the houses on the block. The old block. There was the avenue, the factory walls, and our street. Our street was something special. I should have spent much more time on our street, exploring, taking advantage of it. I should have gone back to see my friends, and also the people I had worked with. I had meant to, God knows; the intentions had been good. Yes, everything had vanished. Everything. It was strange, this feeling of regret, this bitterness that I felt as though it were coming from my stomach. I had seen so many things. Rifles, raised fists, hands outstretched, salutes of every kind. It was touching. There hadn't been enough variety in the life I had been leading, sequestered there in my apartment. I had spent an endless number of boring hours there. I thought of Yvonne—or Marie—and applauded her decision to leave. . . . How right she had been! I had carried her suitcases downstairs myself, I had helped the driver load them into the trunk. I still remembered it as though it were yesterday. Which goes to prove that my memory isn't so bad after all. What else did I remember? What else was there to remember? Oh, yes, there was that school teacher, actually the head of the school, a man with grizzled hair and a black mustache. "I pulled myself up by my own bootstraps," he used to say to me, "I'm a self-made man." Then, seated behind his desk: "You'll never amount to anything, my boy. Mark my words. I won't be there any longer, but mark my words well: you'll never amount to anything!"

It was true. Then, addressing his words to my mother but pointing his forefinger right at me, he said: "He'll never amount to anything, Madame," his hard, heartless words stripping away her every illusion, despite the tears in her eyes.

What I felt more than anything else was something missing. If only I had known how to put each moment to good use, life would have been beautiful. I had let the stream of life flow past; I had wasted it, not taken advan-

The Hermit : **165**

tage of it. In any event, it would have been over. But the memories that remained were becoming like paintings in the frames of memory. Paintings that were slightly blurred, darkened to some degree by so many lapses. These memory lapses were like dark spots that concealed the picture. Something had always been missing. I had the feeling anyway that something was missing, which is to say that the missing element or elements were all. What was missing? What was it that I lacked? I wanted to know everything. That's what was missing: the fact that I didn't know. The fact that I didn't know everything. I was ignorant, but not enough for me to realize that I was. What about the scholars and wise men: do they know something? And if they do, is it enough for them? What else is there? Maybe the trees know more. Animals know a lot. I hadn't tried very hard, because I felt that it was impossible to know what I wanted to know. When I came to that conclusion I was unconsolable. Maybe one day people will know. Other people will know all there is to know. That feeling of fatigue that always weighed so heavily on me had stemmed from that inability to know, that impotence. Yes, all those billions and billions of people. There have been billions of people born into this world, and each has been saddled with the universal anxiety. Each one, like Atlas, has had to support the full weight of the world as though he or she were all alone, overwhelmed by the burden of the unknowable. Was it any consolation to me to say to myself that the most learned man in the world was just as ignorant as I, and that he was the first to realize it? But is that true?

One day I was awakened by the chirping of birds. I opened my window and saw that a tree, an all-white tree in full flower, had grown as high as my window. One of its branches was so close I could reach out and touch it. Blue birds and green birds took flight from its branches, then settled back on the tree, a tree unlike any I had ever seen before. It had taken root in the pile of garbage in the courtyard that had itself been transformed into a lawn of grass. It had a smooth trunk, above which was the crown of branches and flowers that opened at the level of my window. I reached out and plucked three immaculate flowers.

"Come and see," I shouted, "come and see what I've found!"

The words echoed emptily in the apartment. The concierge knocked gently at my door. I opened it. I noted that she was already beginning to show signs of age.

"Come and see the beautiful tree that's grown up in the courtyard," I said. "It grew in the space of a single night. Come and see, if you don't believe me. Do you hear the birds?"

"I don't hear a thing." she said.

With great reluctance she headed toward the window.

"What are you telling me?" she said. "There isn't any tree."

I looked out the window, and indeed the tree had disappeared.

"Then what about those flowers I picked off one of its branches! Look, there they are. I put them on the table."

She looked at them closely. "Yes, they're flowers all right. I've never seen any quite like them. Where did they come from?"

"From the tree. The tree I was just telling you about!"

Again she looked at the three flowers. She put them in a glass of water and left without another word, simply shrugging her shoulders.

I was disappointed. Where could that tree have gone? And yet it had been there a little while before, I had the three flowers to prove it. I touched them, smelled them. The concierge had seen them with her own eyes. I was astonished but reassured, too. I resumed my station at the window. There was a kind of trembling in the walls and ceiling that surrounded me, luminous vibrations in the blinding light. The walls and the roof seemed to be breaking up; their lines became blurred. They lost their density and seemed to me to turn into something extremely fragile. Now they were mere curtains, increasingly transparent, penumbras, evanescent shadows. I saw them sway gently to the left, then to the right, trembling like images in running water, then I saw them shrivel up and slowly recede into the distance. They melted like so much transparent smoke into the luminous distance, then disappeared. Before my eyes, the desert stretched, vast beneath the brilliant sky, the burning sun, to the very horizon. There was no longer anything but sand sparkling in the light. My room seemed to be suspended, silent, a tiny dot in all that immensity.

This was preceded by a long moment of silence: stretched out on my bed, I stared at the closet against the far walls, with its double doors. The doors swung open. They seemed to be two big gates. I couldn't see any clothing now, nor any linen. Only the bare wall. Now the wall disappeared in turn. The doors, wide-open, turned into two gilded columns which were supporting a very tall pediment. Where the wall had been, images began to form and slowly reform. It grew very bright. A tree crowned with flowers and leaves appeared. Then another. Several. A long pathway. At the end, a light brighter than daylight. The light came nearer, encompassing everything. How could my room contain it? It was far bigger than the room. I couldn't feel the wind that coursed through the branches and rustled the leaves and the blue and white flowers. Yes, I could, a gentle breeze. It was a meadow. How lovely the meadow was! Who was it for? Who was this meadow, this garden, this light for? The trees, in perfect rows, stretched into the distance. Between them, in the foreground, a tree sprang up. A tree or a big bush? To its right, that is to my left, a silver ladder, whose base stood a good three feet off the ground, rose and disappeared into the blue sky.

For a long time I went on watching, afraid to get up, to approach the scene, for fear it would vanish. I could have touched that bush; I could have touched that ladder. The light was very bright, and yet it did not hurt my eyes. The rungs of the ladder shone brightly. The garden came toward me, surrounded me, I was in it, part of it. Years passed, or seconds. The ladder came toward me. It hovered just above my head. Years passed, or seconds. It began to recede, to melt. The ladder disappeared, then the bush, then the trees. Then the columns with the triumphal arch. Some part of that light that had entered into me remained.

I took that for a sign.